UMBERTO

A MAFIA ROMANCE

COCO MILLER

COCO MILLER ROMANCE

Want to be notified when I release my next book or give away freebies?

JOIN MY LIST

Coco On Facebook

Coco On Instagram

www.CocoMillerRomance.com

LICENSE NOTE

BOOKS BY COCO

Big City Billionaires
Faking For Mr. Pope
Virgin Escort For Mr. Vaughn
Pretending for Mr. Parker

Red Bratva Billionaires
MAXIM
SERGEI
VIKTOR

The Overwatch Division
WYATT
ASA
CESAR

Andolini Crime Family

CARMINE

GIOVANNI

UMBERTO

INTRODUCTION

Caution: The gangster in this love story always gets what he wants, even if he has to take it.

I'm Victoria Holt. Former heir to an empire, current broke college student, and prisoner of Umberto Bova —one of New York's biggest mafia dons. I'm not who he thinks I am, and I'm going to fight to keep it that way. Even if he is one of the hottest and best lovers, I've ever had. Even if I am his captive.

I'm Umberto Lorenzo Bova. As a mafia kingpin, I've made enemies by the dozen and committed unspeakable acts, but I always seem to get what I want. Tonight, the thing I want the most is a beautiful girl I found escaping the cold weather inside a New York coffee shop. She doesn't know that she stopped me from killing a man. She doesn't realize that there's nothing that can stop me from making her mine. I always get what I want. Even if that means kidnapping her.

CHAPTER ONE

Victoria

Being a poor college student stinks. Being a poor college student without a boyfriend sucks even more. It's especially hard when your roommate (aka hoebag) brings home a new guy to have sex with every night, and you are stuck out in the hallway to study. Like I'm a nerdy stray cat, she can just toss out of the house at her leisure.

To top off this train wreck, I'm Victoria Holt, former heiress to Holt luxury hotels. I'm trying to lay low during my years at college because I want people to know me for who I am and not for who my family is. Holt Hotels is a well-known brand with more than five thousand hotels worldwide. We were once famous. Now we are infamous.

I didn't grow up wanting for much, but I did grow up having to work for my family. In the early days, before things really blew up big for my mom and dad's company, I used to help dress beds and clean up rooms. As a teen, I worked counters checking in guests and even as a lifeguard for the pools in the summertime.

I'm not a stranger to working like an average Joe, but after my family was offered a hefty sum of money to be bought out as the owners of the properties, things changed drastically at home for us. For one, my parents, who had a rocky marriage, to begin with, thanks to all the stress and time spent on building the hotels up as a brand, got a divorce not too long after.

This was also part of the reason why they decided to sell and split the money. But after that, things only got worse. My father made several really bad investments and lost a huge chunk of his wealth. Then he became a heavy drinker and spent the rest of his fortune on high-stakes gambling.

To make ends meet he's now a janitor in a local high school even though they constantly write about him in the tabloids and the paparazzi still tirelessly follows him around. They are trying to get a glimpse into the 'fallen' former owner of the world's most exclusive hotel brand's lifestyle as a blue-collar worker. In other words, the press loves to document my father's downfall.

He even did a stint on a reality TV show with one of those pseudo doctors who look like they actually give a damn as they talk to celebs about their sobriety and life choices. That money went fast too, and he never finished the program. After the cameras quit rolling, that so-called doctor didn't give a damn about my father, and we never heard from him again.

My mother made slightly better choices but still never lived up to the name she was once proud of. She spent most of her money investing in a beauty care line created overseas. Sadly for her, it failed miserably thanks to all the negative press surrounding my father, even though they now have two different last names. No one trusted her. She couldn't get her products placed in stores and this was before Instagram ads, so there weren't enough customers buying.

The fact that both of my parents more or less wasted their fortunes meant there was nothing left when it came time to pay for my college. I am not some rich kid celebrity who has had everything handed to them and tried to look normal by flinging myself into some university to get a degree in liberal arts or history or some other dumb shit like that. No offense, but if the shoe fits, wear it. I'm actually serious about becoming a doctor.

I want to build a name for myself that is strong enough, so if anyone were to ever speak badly of me or my name, they'd know it was all a lie based on my reputation, not my family. I want to help people and be a good woman. I want to stand on my own two feet. But currently, I am locked out of my damn room and sitting in the loud ass hallway of the dorms as I try to cram for a test I have early in the morning.

This is one time in my life that I wish I could actually pull clout and use my name. Too bad, my name doesn't have as much power behind it as it once did. Where it used to demand respect and meant people listened to my every word; now it is synonymous with what not to do for the rich and famous.

I'll be honest with you. My roommate is such a bitch, and there's nothing I can do about it unless I want to sit in there and listen to her fuck a new guy every night. Which I absolutely do not want to do. Obviously.

On top of all of this, I am starving to death. I

think the last time I ate was two years ago. I'm not even kidding. I'm trying this new diet I heard about called intermittent fasting, and it means I have to fast for like twelve hours or something between meals.

I honestly feel like my stomach is eating my other organs. I am that damn hungry. My friend from biology class swears by it though, and she definitely has the body to prove it must work, but shit, I am a hungry little mess. I'm so hungry I would eat stalks of celery, but even that is not allowed during the fasting period. I think 97% of all foods are not allowed on this diet, truthfully. It sure as hell feels that way at least.

Thankfully coffee is allowed. I scoop up all of my books and my bag and sling them inside the door, and then head off to the place that funds me this great slab of carpet in the hallway, AKA my job, at the local little coffee shop near my school. That's right; I make coffee to earn my way through life.

I make money honestly and thankfully working there means throwing on a baseball hat and being able to hide who I am. The owner is super trendy AKA weird and makes us all wear name tags with fake names she creates for us. I'm actually thankful for it, honestly.

My name at work is Destiny. I had to laugh a

little the day she pinned the badge on my lime green apron. But in truth, No Tea No Shade— I love that name—makes me feel like I have something to live up to.

It's freezing outside already. I've always loved New York but damn the cold weather in the Fall and Winter makes me dream of white sand beaches and iced fruity drinks to sip on under the heat of the summertime sun. I have on a sweater dress and leggings with flats, and baby, that does little keep out the bone-chilling air whipping around me. I didn't think to grab more than this or my coat before I was basically tossed out of my dorm, though. It will have to do.

I have to walk past my former stomping grounds just make it to the coffee shop. The hotel I grew up in is decorated beautifully in festive bronze and red colors as I pass by, recalling the memories of my childhood. I look back at it, remembering all the good and bad times I spent there as I stroll by it. It was the first hotel we ever owned and ran ourselves.

My father used his inheritance from my grandfather, who was a farmer in his day, to buy it. He's long gone now, but he had left my dad a hefty sum that he had saved up his entire life. It's a pity to know that it has all been for nothing. It's something that I can't quite forgive my father for just yet.

It feels like he has just let so many of us down. I pray for him every Sunday in church. I also pray that one day it will actually work, and God will hear me and save him from himself. But until then, I'm on my own to deal with things.

The front door of the coffee shop is decorated in fake snow and a big fat snowman on the glass of the door. The owner who will only answer to her chosen name 'Starbright' says we can only put snowmen on the door because it's wrong to objectify people and by 'people' she means Santa Clause—a made-up character.

The woman is just way too damn extra, but she's also sweet and pays me to work for her, so who am I to judge. At least her brand of crazy is protecting people, even if they are made up of fictional beings from children's stories. It's still better than the alternative.

I thank God once I'm inside the warm space of the coffee shop and hurry to the counter to grab a hot cup of coffee. My favorite girl to work with is here. She's this little redheaded Irish girl who is barely five feet tall but takes shit from nobody. She is a little badass, and we get along like sisters.

Her birth name is Racheal, but in the shop, during working hours, she is 'Glimmer'. I know, it sounds ridiculous, but the girl owns it. I can't hate on her at all. She even started wearing liquid eyeshadow with glittering flakes and matching lip gloss just to make a statement about it. I about died. Starbright thought it was a real moment, telling her she is finally becoming 'her true self'. Ha. Whatever the hell that means, beats me.

Glimmer sees me and brightens up.

"Hey Victoria girl," she says with a big smile. She has on electric blue gloss and shimmering eyeshadow today and against her fiery red head of hair looks like the damn Fourth of July.

I don't say anything though. She can look any damn way she pleases. The way she kind of pulls it off, makes me a little envious of her too. I'm more of a natural pallet type of chick. I like my bronzers and highlighters. If you can call a bright yellow highlighter natural on my skin, that is. A fierce red lip moment is about as brave as I get with my look, and that is usually reserved for special occasions, not every day latte-making wear.

"Hey, Racheal. How's it going today?"

"I'm gonna take a stab and say my day is going

better than yours. Roomy kick you out for the D again?"

"Girl, I'm about ready to go old school and *literally* drag a bitch out of that room."

Racheal laughs. "You could always come and stay at my place."

"You have fifty cats and no windows in that cell you call an apartment. Plus, it's way too far from campus. You know I like to sleep in a little on cold mornings. I'd never make it to class on time."

"True," she giggles. "But the offer is there if you need it. Until then, how about I make you a pumpkin spice latte?"

"Ugh, I'm still on that diet. I need something full fat, no sugar."

"I can hook you up." She smiles and gets to work. "You look great, by the way."

"Thanks. I hate losing weight though. I mean, I love it, but the first thing to go is always my boobs and butt. And girl, I need those things."

"Haha, can't relate. I've always been the Tin Man." She models her super flat board-like body that is like a teenage boy rather than a woman in her 20's.

"It works for you though."

Someone behind me clears his throat. I quickly swivel my head to see what the hell is up. It's a man with a black button-down shirt pushed up to his elbows and a grey tie looped perfectly around his thick neck. The shirt clings to his frame, accentuating every muscle on his firm body.

"Sorry," he says, "I just couldn't help but overhear your conversation. I wanted to say that I think both of you ladies would be any man's dream girl."

Racheal laughs. "Oh, baby thanks, but this girl only likes girls." She winks at him, and his grin grows wider. "Sadly Victoria does not, so I can't have her. Keep hitting on her though. She needs someone. Bad!"

"Racheal!" I warn, cutting her to bits with my stare. Realizing that we've just both used our real names out loud and not our barista names.

The mystery man turns to me. "I'm only offering a compliment." His voice dips low. "But if you want more . . ." He doesn't finish the sentence, and I raise my brow.

"You'd be willing to give me what? The promise to be my boyfriend, and your number? Is that what you're suggesting? Damn mister man, we haven't even had coffee yet."

"Maybe we should then?"

CHAPTER TWO

Victoria

I scoff at hot guy's offer, but honestly, I laugh at it too. I'm actually giving him snaps for going there so bravely and boldly with me.

Who is this guy? I mean, *really?* He's pretty damn good looking I'll give him that. And he smells just as rich as his watch suggests he is. I bet he never gets kicked out into the hallway or out of anywhere. I bet he owns more than most of the people he meets in a day.

He could probably buy me.

What the hell am I saying? This man isn't even my type. It must be his hypnotic gaze. He has expressive chocolate brown eyes seem to melt as we stay staring at each other in the middle of the coffee shop. That I work at.

Damn it.

Get it together, girl.

I clear my throat as I try to snap back to reality, pulling myself from his powerful stare. I take a deep breath and say more confidently, "I'm not looking to hook up with anyone for any reason right now. I'm focused on school, and that is all. But thank you. I think."

The hottie smiles. "What are you studying?"

Racheal slinks up to us and holds my arm. "Why don't you two find somewhere more cozy to sit, and I'll bring you some coffee?"

"Listen here little miss Glimmer . . ." I start to protest, but the hot guy offers his elbow, and I stupidly take hold of him.

I'm instantly regretting my choice once I do because daaaaamn he feels good. Just holding on to his freaking elbow has me catching feelings. Mostly in my Victoria's Secret panties. But still. Feelings are feelings.

My swollen bud comes to life as we walk to the table. Between listening to my roommate get her freak on every night and getting hit on for the first time since never, I think my body is overreacting to his presence.

Mystery man pulls my chair out for me to sit before taking the seat right next to me, pressing his large warm male frame up against my petite shivering body. He notices and rustles around until he finds his coat on a rack near the door, stepping back over to me to wrap it around my shoulders. Then he starts to rub his hands up and down my arms, so the friction warms me up. Like a gentleman straight out of a sweet Disney fairytale or Nicholas Sparks movie.

Racheal brings us over our steaming mugs of coffee and smiles hugely before she trots off. I look over to my mystery man, and he seems just fine sitting here, sipping coffee with a total stranger.

I imagine a man like him is probably used to getting things his way. He reaches forward and grabs his mug, flashing his sparkling designer watch again as he brings the cup to his lips. His jawline could cut glass. He has dark hair shading his cheeks and chin with just the right amount of stubble. Maybe two or three days at best of not shaving. I really like it. My lady parts like it even more. Like I said, I'm horny as hell.

"So...what's your name?" I ask him.

The man swallows, and then wipes his mug with a napkin like he's erasing his mouth print on the lip of the mug.

"My friends call me Enzo, but I was born Umberto Lorenzo Bova."

What a beautiful name.

"Are you famous or something?"

He looks like an actor.

"Not at all."

"Oh, I could have sworn I've heard that name before."

Umberto shrugs. "What's your name?"

"Depends who you ask," I laugh.

"I'm asking you," he says seriously.

"Well, I was born Victoria, but when I work at this fine coffee-drinking establishment, I am only known as a barista named Destiny."

He snorts. "Whose lame fuckin' rule is that?"

"The owner. Her name is Starbright."

"Okay, now you're just having fun with me, aren't you?"

"Nope. That's on God."

"Do you have a last name Victoria?"

"I think I'm going to keep that to myself, for now."

"Interesting...but I guess I can't say much. I have... colleagues... that use nicknames too."

"Oh yeah? Like what?" I take a sip of coffee, and his intense gaze comes back as he looks at me.

"I'd tell you, but it would get us killed. You don't want that now do you?"

"You must know some pretty bad people, then." I take a deep breath.

"You know how I said my friends call me Enzo? That was kind of a joke. I don't have friends. I'm not in the friend-making kind of business."

I smile. "I'll be your friend."

He smiles too, but it's all wrong. Like I'm a foolish girl that he pities. "That's sweet, Victoria, and I'd be honored, except men like me don't have friends. We're incapable."

My heart hammers in my chest at how he looks at me. He looks deadly when he stares with so much intensity, and his voice dips a couple of octaves sounding like a midnight train.

"Why not?" I ask, braving the question.

He leans closer for a moment. "Because I'm a dangerous man and being friends with me wouldn't be in your best interest."

I can't tell if he's joking. "Are . . . Are you going to hurt me?"

Umberto squints his eyes a little as he thinks over my words silently to himself. He scans over my body as he appraises how I look in his dark heavy coat that must be made of cashmere or something else equally as delectable and soft. The coat hugs me like a glove and keeps me toasty warm. It smells just like him too but with a hint of something else. I can pick up a touch of leather, but there is another element that eludes me. Something deep within the fibers, much like Umberto.

And honestly, it's driving me a bit insane.

Yeah, I'm definitely horny.

CHAPTER THREE

Umberto

"That's a very hard question to answer." I eye her, trying not to scare her off with my words. I can't help myself. She is such a strikingly beautiful girl, and unlike any woman I've ever had before.

I first saw her from this very spot, while sitting here watching the space around me. I've been waiting for that fuck Dema to make his way out of the damn bathroom, so I could pop him three blocks down the street where no one would ever know his body was dumped in the alleyway.

I overheard this pretty little thing talking to her cute little Irish girlfriend at the counter. Both girls talking about themselves as if they either of them couldn't get any man in New York City to fuck them freely. Why do girls think like that? They are as fine as it gets and still think they can't grab any man's attention. Let's get real. It boils my blood. What dickhead in their past led them to believe that they aren't worthy of someone singing praises? That they aren't worthy of being told how drop-dead fucking gorgeous they are every day?

Especially this one in front of me.

This girl is a diamond amongst pebbles. I'd spot her in the middle of an epic sea of women she's so damn pretty. And hot. Her body is like a twisted road of curves and hills. Thick and curvy in all the right places. That damn sweater dress hugs her tits just right, and she has an ass most women dream of having. Her legs are encased in skin-tight leggings, leaving little to my imagination. I'm caught up in her gorgeous face and starlit eyes, filled with the ocean as she blinks at me. The flecks of blue in her eyes is vastly striking against the deep color of her skin.

I've never been with a girl like her, but damn it, I'd love to. I need to know what that ass feels like sitting on my face as I smack it until she cries out my name. Her tits need to be sucked on, and I can only imagine what her snatch must feel and taste like. If it's anything like the intoxicating scent on her skin, I'm a dead man already.

Forget Dema. Bastard got lucky. He won't be dying tonight because this girl has captured the attention of my Grim Reaper alter ego. Speaking of fuckin Dema, he still hasn't made it out of the bathroom, which leads me to believe he spotted me and probably bolted out a window or some shit. The motherfucker. When I get my hands on him, I swear, I'm gonna fuck him up royally. I need to find him first though. That lowlife owes *me* money. This is what happens when you let junkies do your dirty work for you. Eventually, they decide it's okay to let one person get away without paying me what's owed. And if I let one of them get away with it, they will all think it's okay, and that's just bad business. So sometimes, you just gotta do shit yourself.

I'm about to grab up this girl and swoon my way into getting her in the backseat of my car when a camera is suddenly thrust into our faces as a woman shouts questions in our direction. I'm about to pull out my Glock and tell her to get the fuck out of my face when I hear what she's actually asking. She's pointing the questions in Victoria's direction. Being an heir to the Holt empire? Holt Hotels? That damn family? That's her last name?

It can't be.

Victoria didn't tell me her last name was Holt.
What the fuck? You've got to be kidding me. Did I
just hit the damn lottery? Is she the long lost
daughter of Dema Holt? The gambler who doesn't
pay his bills. The fucker I'm looking for?

Surely her ass backwards parents set her up with
a trust fund before blowing through their money.
Why would his daughter be working in a coffee shop
where the flakey ass owner makes her change her
name to some hippy-dippy shit? This reporter lady
has to be wrong.

"Is it true that your father isn't really broke?" the
woman asks, shoving her camera phone in Victoria's
face. "What are his plans now that Holt Hotels is
back up for sale? Will he take the owner up on his
offer to take back the reigns?"

Victoria sits upright in her seat. "My family is
none of your concern. I'd appreciate it if you would
leave me alone."

But the woman keeps hammering on, and I see
how uncomfortable Victoria is, which only pisses me
off. I stand. My frame easily towers over the tiny
woman with the camera.

"Why don't you leave her alone? Clearly, she
doesn't want to answer your questions. I think you

better respect her wishes, or else you'll have some serious problems on your hands."

"Oh! Are you her bodyguard? Do you still have money left for a bodyguard, Victoria? Is your dad paying for that?"

"Why don't we move you somewhere less . . . crowded, Victoria?" I offer her my hand and help her navigate her way to the door, so the annoying camera lady won't get in our way. The last thing I need is media attention. I thrive in the dark, and in the dark is where I wish to remain.

She feels like an angel in my arms. So naturally, I lead her to hell. I have a club not too far from here. One of the classiest joints you'll see bare tits in the city. I'm not even in it for the T & A. I'm in it for the cash. I'm in it for the cover of what a cash business like a strip club does for my money game. I'm not about making money that can be traced or books that need to be kept honestly. I don't do taxes, and I damn sure don't do other people taking what's mine.

I hustle for my money, and so does everyone in the Andolini Crime Family. This club is our money haven. It's how we keep our shit clean and the FEDS off our asses. For the most part anyhow. It might not be the best place to take a classy girl like Victoria, but it provides protection for us, because there isn't a damn person dumb enough to try and come up in my club gunning for me or anyone I know without an invitation. And that damn press lady or anyone else from the lame news media sure as fuck would never be able to step foot into my cash cleaning empire. My doorman will see to that.

Victoria walks close to my side as we enter through a special entrance, only I can use, bypassing security and the bullshit of the main room. I wrap a protective arm around her shoulders as we cut through the rows of tables and clients as they drink and enjoy the show. I find the door to my office and take a seat on the edge of my desk, allowing Victoria to have the plush white sofa. She takes off my jacket, revealing her tight body and settles in. I don't dare sit close to her again. I don't trust myself not to fuck her right here in my office, and I don't do that shit where I work. Playtime is for any number of hotels around the city. This is where I work and work only.

My assistant Karlita stops dead in her high heeled tracks as soon as she sees what's happening in my office. Her mouth drops to a perfect 'O' shape, and I have to give her the 'don't fuck with me' stare in order to keep everything in line. I don't need to scare poor Victoria any more than I already have by telling her that shit about not having friends and being a dangerous man. But she needs to know that I am not good. I am not the kind of guy you bring home to mom and dad.

"I didn't think you were coming back tonight, Mr. Bova," Karlita says quickly. "I was just going to drop off the numbers, sir."

"Plans changed a little," I tell her, tightening my expression. "I'm going to see to it that this girl finds her way home. She's having a little trouble with the press. Apparently, she's a big deal in this city."

"Oh," Victoria says, "I'm not. That lady is just confused."

I squint my eyes curiously. "I somehow don't believe that."

"Shall I call the car, Sir?" Karlita asks, her eyes looking a bit unsure.

"Yes, that would be good, Karlita. Tell them to park around back."

"Yes, Sir. I will get that in order right away, Mr. Bova."

"Thank you, Karlita."

She leaves us alone.

"Are you really taking me home? I only live a few blocks away from here, and I don't want to be trouble."

"Yes, I am. No one is going to bother you

tonight." No one except for me. "Were you warm enough in the jacket you had on or would you prefer a heavier one. It's getting rather cold out, and you're not nearly equipped in that skimpy little number you have on to keep warm. What were you thinking?"

I slip my arms out of my suit jacket and hold it up for her. Victoria stands and slips her skinny arms into the holes and then fucking hums as she turns around.

"Smells like a dream."

"Excuse me?" I ask. "What smells like a dream?"

"Your coat," she says, taking another sniff at the sleeve. "Your jacket smells really good. And it's really warm." She sighs. "I kind of get kicked out of my dorm a lot. I have a nymphomaniac for a roommate. I'm studying to be a doctor, and all my study time is basically spent in the hallway. But tonight, I was trying to find somewhere a little comfier to relax after studying. I didn't think to grab my coat before I was tossed out like a stray cat."

I stare at her petite frame up against my large body. Victoria moves closer, putting her fingers on my red tie, stroking it with her touch as she slides the silk through her fingers and stares up at me with those bedroom eyes of hers. She's batting her long dark lashes like blinking fast will cast some kind of fucking magic spell over my ass. And maybe they do because when she looks up at me all innocently like this, I want to lean into her and kiss the shit out of her perfect little mouth.

It takes every ounce of discipline I have learned in my life, doing all kinds of illegal dirty deeds as one of New York's most wanted gangsters, to not toss her pretty ass across my desk and fuck her right here and now.

I cannot fuck in my office. That is a big fucking red X. No, I won't do it. But goddamn it would be hot.

"Need something from me, Victoria?" I ask, allowing my hands to fall on her wide hips, which is a really dumb fucking idea.

She trembles, and I feel my dick twitch inside my pants.

Stay focused motherfucker. Stay fucking focused.

"I'm really grateful to you for helping me, Umberto," Victoria almost whispers. Pressing closer, she tips up on her toes and kisses my cheek.

I try to duck away, but the damage is done, and it's too fucking late. My heart already starts to beat to a new and unfamiliar rhythm that really confuses the hell out of me. The worst part of any plan going south is becoming the one getting screwed over instead of the one doing the screwing, and I am a righteous fucking screwer of plans. Right now, I feel pretty damn screwed as she touches me with her softness and kindness. My body repels such shit. As if I could be so easily taken over by this girl dressed like a starving college student... wearing my damn coat.

Ugh, it will smell just like her heavenly scent now, too. She is like breathing in a field of wildflowers mixed with vanilla ice cream. My hardening cock begs to know what she feels like. I want full relief of this pain, this need, but shit, I'd settle for a sample of her mouth, too. She must have felt how hard I am beneath my pants because she grinds into me a bit with her belly, and then smiles shyly.

"I'm sorry. I should not have done that."

I raise a brow. "No, you shouldn't have done that at all. You're in for it now, baby."

"I usually don't hook up with guys like this," she whispers. "But you're just so . . ." My grip on her hips tightens, and she gasps; her sweet breath fanning my face, seducing me further.

"I'm just so what, Victoria?"

"You just make me feel so different than any guy I've been around before."

"Most men aren't like me, baby. They don't play by the rules I play by."

"And what rules are those, Umberto Bova?"

"I make the rules," I growl. "And I break the rules. I'd never let anyone toss you out of anywhere. And I'll have any motherfucker who ever treats you with such disrespect handled properly and swiftly."

She likes what I've said. It turns her on.

"I think I need you tonight, Umberto."

"Then baby, I'm going to give you what you want. What you need."

I slide my hands up her hips to her waist and rest them by her collar. She feels exquisite.

But this is Dema's damn daughter and she's young and probably perfectly innocent of all of his bullshit. Should I do this?

Her eyes flutter as I trace one of my fingers along the side of her neck and my decision is simple.

"Open up for me, baby."

CHAPTER FOUR

Umberto

Victoria slowly complies, allowing me to slide my thumb between her plump, glossy lips and finger fuck the shit out of her mouth as she swirls her tongue around it. I get harder as I watch her swirl her tongue on the pad of my thumb and push it as deep into her throat as I can without her gagging. Goddamn it that's so fucking hot.

She hums hungrily for more. I give in and grasp her head tightly in my hands, tipping that pretty face of hers up to me so I can thrash my hungry tongue against hers, delving deep into her mouth as if it were a viper trying to strike.

We stumble as the kiss deepens and ignites into an inferno, unlike anything I have ever felt before. Every fiber in my being pulls me toward her for more, and that is not even enough. I want to crawl inside her molecules and take up residence beneath her ribcage.

There is something that lives in this girl that wants to bring me back from the dead, and it lives inside her kiss. I could come right where I stand as she touches me with her soft hands, and I feel her delicious skin.

"It's your lucky day," I growl into her ear. "I'm gonna make you come with my fingers as I fuck that sweet cunt. Then I'm going to fuck you all night with my dick."

I take my time removing my coat from her and easing her leggings down her body, kissing every inch of flesh exposed.

"Oh my God," she cries out as I shove two fingers between her wet pussy lips, barely able to fit inside her because she's so hot and tight around my fingers.

I roll her swollen clitoris with my free fingers and shove her against the desk opening her legs wide. I take a small taste of that slick, slippery pussy, and it's as good as a fine wine. But dammit, Karlita is probably going to be back any minute now to tell me the car is ready and waiting for us.

I pummel Victoria's tight little snatch with my fingers, not letting her up until she loses her breath inside my mouth as I smother her with my kiss. She clenches her walls around me as I find just the right spot deep in her pussy and fuck her until she comes.

"Umberto! Oh, I'm coming, I'm coming," she cries out, swirling her wide hips to get me even deeper like the little vixen she is. I am so hard it is painful.

"This pussy is all mine tonight," I growl. "I'm going to fuck you so good."

"More," Victoria demands as she rocks on my hand to reach the height of her orgasm.

I fucking love to watch all of it ... how she's so brave to get off on my fingers. I'm a damn stranger practically. And after I told her I was dangerous, too. It means she trusts me. Fuck yes. I need that. Her pebbled nipples brush up against my chest, and I am so engorged I could explode.

"Oh, holy fuck, Umberto," she pants heavily. "I can't believe we did this." She cups her mouth. "I never do things like this. I swear."

"Well, I guess you do now, pretty girl and I'm

happy to be the first." I pull away from her and catch my breath, trying to calm down my dick.

"Who knew that the quiet Italian man I met in a coffee shop would have such a big dick and finger fuck me so good," she murmurs. I don't think I was supposed to hear that, but it makes me laugh.

I grab my crotch firmly and raise a brow. "You've never been fucked by a stallion like me, baby. I can tell you've never had that sweet snatch gobbled up by a proper man have you?"

"I've never been with someone like you, no," the little tease admits to me, with that damn shyness returning to her gorgeous eyes. "Although you have me seriously curious about all the possibilities, Umberto."

"You're a greedy little girl tonight, aren't you? Just can't get enough."

"I shouldn't be saying this but yeah, you promised me all night and that's what I want."

"It's okay to tell me what you want," I say quietly. " I love a woman who knows what she wants and is so beautiful." I play my finger across her full lips. "These eyes, these lips, that pussy. Damn that pussy is so delicious. It still wants me to fuck it, doesn't it?"

"Yes," she practically begs, her chest heaving,

making her huge tits call to me. I palm the left one and squeeze, pinching her nipple with a little tug. She cries out, and I almost groan.

"Fuck, you are so damn hot. I want those big titties on my face and around my dick right now. I'm going to shoot my cum all over your pretty hard nipples."

"I'm so wet right now," she pants. "No one has ever made me feel this before, Umberto. I'm aching for you."

"Spread your legs, pretty girl. I want what you've been dying to give to me. That pussy. I have to fuck you, right this instant," I demand.

Victoria turns her hot fucking body toward me, and then kneels at the edge of the huge desk as I stand before her, my hefty cock finally free from my pants and standing at full attention for her yearning wet mouth.

"Let me suck you off first, Umberto. Don't want you to come too fast. I need you inside me for a long time." My hungry pretty girl darts her sexy and sweet tongue out quickly, licking the precum off the tip of my hard cock.

For a fleeting moment I think about who this is. This isn't just some random chick I'm banging the shit out of. She's Dema's daughter. This could get complicated...or not. I decide not to make it complicated and focus on the situation in front of me instead. Victoria on her knees.

She is working hard to please me and swallows the head of my thick rod with one fell swoop. I groan loudly, but I don't even care who hears at this point. I am so far gone. Completely off the fucking reservation. This girl has made me crazed with the need and desire for her. That's all the monster inside of me sees and wants. Her. Victoria fucking Holt.

"Take that dick, baby. Suck me hard."

"Shit, you're so big, I can barely fit all of you in my mouth." But like a good girl, she takes me to the hilt every damn time she goes back for more.

"You're doing just fine, pretty girl."

I grasp her head and shove my cock into her throat. "Take me all the way, yes, like that, princess. Fuck me deep with your mouth. All the way to my balls. Yes, just like that. Just fucking like that. It's so damn good."

"Mmm, yes." She hums around my dick as I thrust my hips deep into her. Victoria's hands land on my ass, and she pulls me deep, looking up into my face with those electric eyes of hers.

"You are so damn sexy, Victoria." I pull away from her, and a long stream of saliva leaks out of her mouth and down across her tits. I wipe it away and pull her up by her arms, pressing my lips against hers as I fuck her mouth with my tongue this time.

"You want this big Italian cock to fuck you good, don't you?"

"Badly," she admits. "I can't take it anymore. I need you inside of me."

I attack her mouth again, and she swings her leg over my hip. The tip of my hard cock brushes her swollen lips and clit, and we both moan at the same time at how close we are and how damn good that shit feels. Fuck, it is so good. Like a dream.

She's puffy and tight as I roam her with my fingers, shoving my long middle finger inside of her tight little caramel box. I spin her quickly around and expose her bare ass cheeks. Then shove her across my desk, not giving a shit about the papers that go flying.

I tug on her big hips and pull her ass up in that air before slapping each cheek until she is mewling for my dick. I taste her again, this time sinking my tongue deep into her pussy as I lick it from the back, all the way up to her second hole, and then make the circuit again.

"Beg me." I tap my cock on her perfect ass cheek and wiggle my fingers across her clit.

"*Please*, Umberto, fuck me right now."

"You like to be spanked like a bad girl, don't you?" I swat my hand to the apple of her ass, and she cries out.

"Ooh, Yes. Yes, baby. Just like that."

Damn she's hot.

I shove my dick in her entrance, and she pushes onto it, sliding that slick sopping wet cunt down my shaft until I am seated deep inside of her. I let her work me because watching that plump ass of hers has me all kinds of fucking twisted up. She knows how to ride a dick. That's for damn sure.

She's fucking me so good, I can hardly take being a bystander in this event. I slap my hands on her ass and start to slide them up her body until I wrap my fingers around the column of her throat as I work my hips, slamming into her from the back. Beating that sweet pussy up until she's constricting around me as tightly as a fucking damn Boa. I've never done anything hotter in my life, and that's saying a hell of a fucking lot, considering my long record with fucking women.

"Shit," I grunt. "I'm going to fucking come."

"Come in my mouth," she demands. Surprising me yet again. God, she's hot.

Victoria swings herself around and falls back to

her knees. I steadily fuck her mouth, and she keeps popping her mouth on and off my thick head, toying with the head of my cock until it's too much, and I come long and hard in her mouth.

"You perfect girl." I smack her round thick ass hard. "Fuck, that was amazing. Let's get the fuck outta here and forget our problems for a while, yeah?"

"That sounds nice." Victoria nods wiping her mouth.

I help her adjust her clothes and make sure she is wrapped up nice and warm in my heavy jacket again.

"I've got a nice spot I want to take you to. Do you like good drinks and music?"

"Dancing? Hell, yes. I love it."

"Good."

We dash off in the Cadillac, ignoring security as they try to stop me before I go. Fuck it. I don't want to deal with anyone but this woman tonight. I feel free finally, like a new man with her.

"Who was that?" Victoria asks about the security as we speed through traffic.

I laugh, feeling freer than ever. "Just some people who work for me. It's not a big deal. I'm always in trouble for something. It's part of being with a man like me; you better get used to it."

She raises one eyebrow in a quizzical fashion.

"I'm not exactly meant for a life on the run."

"I'm not running," I scoff. "I'm doing whatever the fuck I want because I can."

She swallows hard. "I didn't mean to insult you."

"It's fine. Let's just have some fun tonight, get to know each other, okay?"

Victoria laughs.

"What?"

"I think we are a little beyond getting to know each other after that fuck fest in your office, that's all."

"You know my cock, not me. And truthfully, that's only a sample of what I have to offer you, pretty girl."

She smiles like the sexy little vixen she is. "I look forward to the main course, then."

"That's what I'm talking about, baby."

I take us to one of my favorite hotels that has a busy bar and lounge inside. Ironically it's a Holt hotel. It's a little pricier than I'd normally pay for to fuck a girl in, but Victoria isn't just anyone, she is something special.

Sometimes I wish I could just get away from all

the pressure and bullshit of having this kind of fucked-up life. Even though I do enjoy most parts of it, I'm always in danger or threatening someone else's life. It's something I was born into. I didn't really have a choice.

There is a party happening out on the patio area of the bar and it looks to be lamer than any scene I'd normally be found at, but Victoria looks all excited about it, and I'm not about to bring down her happiness.

"It's a nice vibe in here, Umberto." Victoria pulls on my arm. "Come dance with me. This is such a great song."

A really loud pop song is playing, and I am not drunk enough to partake in this kind of fuckery, but Victoria is hot as hell, and I smile big at her because I can't help myself.

I laugh. "This isn't my scene. I'm not a dancing type of guy, in case you haven't noticed."

"I have noticed, but I also noticed that you brought me specifically here... so what's that all about?"

"I want to watch you dance. I'm a bit of a voyeur in that way."

She grins playfully, pulling me in closer to her, which my hard cock loves. I get harder as she runs her hands across my chest, but I have to put that feeling to rest for a moment while I try to collect myself and make sure I stay focused on the mission at hand. Regardless of whose fucking daughter she is. Tonight, I am going to have her again and again.

So I watch Victoria drink fruity shit, dance, smile and have a great time under the horrible neon glowing lights as I drink scotch at the hotel's bar. Her eyes eventually drift across the bar to where I am.

I grin at her as she puts on a wild show for me, sexily swaying her wide hips and perfect ass to the beat. I grin right back at her, silently making a note to myself of all the motherfuckers I'm going to kill if they keep looking at her.

They need to know.

Everyone needs to fucking know.

She is *mine*.

CHAPTER FIVE

Victoria

I wake up alone in a fog nestled in a soft bed of white sheets and pillows. Looking around, I realize I'm in a hotel room. Specifically, in the Holt hotel I grew up in. How the fuck did I let that happen?

I was not myself yesterday. I drank way too much last night. I don't want to know what else I did. I can only imagine what Umberto must think of me, letting him do all that nasty stuff. Me doing it return. Well, it wasn't nasty, it was epic. So damn epic.

I've never had an orgasm like the ones he gave to me, and I doubt I ever will again, but I won't do it anymore with him. I have to get back on my game and get my head back into school and my future. A man isn't going to pull me away from my dreams. My destiny. Especially a man like him.

I want to become someone who helps people. Someone who saves people's lives and does not take life away from innocent people. Becoming a doctor is a sure-fire way to do that, and I am going to keep my head on straight and not let anyone get in my path. Even if they are hot as Hades with a fine ass body and a tongue like a viper.

Ugh, I have to stop thinking about it, or else I'll have to douse myself in a tub of cold water just to be able to move. He left me alone in this hotel room, so it probably wasn't as good for him anyway.

Oh, but thinking about the way he ate my pussy and fucked me senseless is like recalling a wet dream, only it really happened. How can a man be so perfect between the sheets like that? As if he was born to please me. He must've had so many women.

Bleh! That is not something I want to think about at all. Damn, what am I doing to myself? I need to get out of this bed. Yes. Get out of bed and take a hot shower, wash all of my sins away from the night with my dream man, grab my clothes, put on some lipstick, and then handle my shit. That's my plan.

I hop up from the bed and storm over to the bathroom door, twisting the knob and charging my way inside like a Viking or some shit, fully intending on completing my mission. But there is a problem. A big freaking problem. Umberto Bova is in the shower, and he is naked as the day he was born.

Damn, he didn't leave.

The fucker grins at me. He didn't even bother to close the shower door. This guy is so crazy. But I guess when you look like an Italian god, why bother, right? He's all soaped up with his dark jet-black hair swooped up into a wet chaotic mess on top of his head. His hand washes his ripped torso as he laughs a little. He has a large black-inked tattoo splayed across his chest that says something in Italian. I can't decipher it without asking, and I'm not about to ask that question right now.

"Well, you just gonna stand there and stare, baby, or are you gonna help me out?"

I gasp at him. "Are you serious? It's like eight in the morning. I haven't even had breakfast yet."

"You're staring at a sausage." He shakes his soapy manhood at me. Oh my God! "Let me feed you, Victoria."

"You are too crazy," I laugh at him. "And I much

prefer bacon over sausage." I close the shower door just as he starts choking.

I laugh harder. Got him good.

At the sink, I wash my face and basically take a quick bird bath to clean myself up enough to be respectable and smelling less like a one-night stand and a bit more like a serious college girl. Although I guess those two things could be the same sometimes. It definitely was for me last night. Crap, I need to stop thinking about it.

I grab my purse and slip on my shoes and slip out the door before Mr. Hottie Pants can try to persuade me to eat any more of his 'sausage.' I rush to the elevator and mash on the button as I beg God to please forgive me for last night and let this damn elevator come already. But as the elevator dings and the silver doors slide open, two armed men step out into the hallway. I'm about to scream and run, but a shot fires from behind me, and they duck down.

"Head down!" Umberto comes flying up behind me and wraps me in a tight hold, turning me away from the gunfire.

I'm starting to feel like I'm in a movie or something. This shit is like being in the middle of the Wild Wild West.

My heart is racing so hard in my chest. Who the

hell are they? Why is Umberto shooting at them, and how did he even know that they were going to be here, coming up this way?

I remember the press thing from last night. People still know who I am despite the fact that I've tried to keep my name out of the media and under wraps. Are they here for me? Does my father owe gambling debts again?

I realize that I may have just cheated death and am about to start crying, but Umberto has other plans. He drags us both back towards a hallway door, where he barricades us in as he reloads.

"Are you okay, Victoria?" He is barely out of breath. He doesn't seem phased in the least by what just happened. Who the hell is this guy? Did I just sleep with some trained assassin or some shit?

Oh, hell no. My luck could not be this damn bad. Bad. He did say that, didn't he? He told me back at the coffee shop, he was a dangerous man. This is what the hell he meant? A killer? And not the friendly wanna-be Edward Cullen type of 'I'm a killer', but the real Netflix documentary series type of killer who has been to jail and actually put bodies in the ground?

What the hell? Who walks into a coffee shop and decides to befriend a college girl just to fuck her senseless and then get her involved in crime and killing? I might just be freaking out though. He could be the good guy. This really could be about my dad's sins and not him.

I look at him Umberto closely this time and not through a lust-filled lens. He raises his brow in almost a challenging way. He's got bad news written all over his deep mysterious eyes and hard stare. There's no way this guy helps people or does good deeds.

This man is a stone-cold killer.

I can feel it.

I know it.

And now I'm stuck in a hotel with him.

My hotel.

"Who are those men?" I ask breathing heavily.

He ignores me as he continues to load and double check his gun. His large body leaning against the door.

"I'm going to hide," I say looking down at the staircase below us.

"Uh-uh. Stay with me."

"I know what I'm doing. I know where to hide."

Hi face changes to one of resolve.

"Okay, if you're sure, go. I'll take care of them and catch up to you later."

CHAPTER SIX

Victoria

When I was little, I loved to hide in the laundry room of the hotel. I don't really know why, but there was something really comforting about being terrified of all the big machines and loud noises but watching everyone work at a frantic pace as if they couldn't even hear the ruckus all around them. It made me feel like the city was not such a scary place.

In New York, there is a constant flow of people, noise, and mayhem. Sometimes that is a welcoming thing; it can entice and ignite you to want to be more and seek adventure and push your limits and comfort zone. But it can also make you feel like I did inside of that laundry room full of chaos—small and unsure about stepping out into the light to face your fears.

The maids didn't seem bothered by anything. They busted ass to just get the job done at any cost, no matter what manager was screaming at them to move faster or if a machine broke down. They took it all in stride, welcoming the challenge.

I think that's where I got my grit from, watching women like them. They made me feel like I could overcome what scared me and do anything I needed to accomplish my goals. Of course, I also loved that they treated me good. They would sneak me cookies and let me build a fort out of clean sheets.

As an adult, I look back and want to kick myself for making them work harder, but they must have done it because they loved me on some level, that they cared about me. I am so grateful that I had women like that in my life because God knows my own mother was always too busy to give me a second look.

I feel that same way again now as I hide out down here barricaded behind the machines and piles of clean linens, waiting for the right time to get out of here. I have no idea where Umberto has gone. I hid here after the fiasco upstairs, and I'm too damn scared to leave this place now that I know there are at least three men in this place who may want to kill me or each other.

How did my life turn from being able to play inside of the halls of this lovely hotel among warm smiling guests and cool as hell staff members, to now hiding out in the dingy laundry room from trained killers?

I need to get out of here, but how? The campus isn't too far away. It's only a few blocks, but what if Umberto follows me? Shit, he already knows where I work. What if he goes after Racheal or crazy ass Starbright? What if it isn't really him, I need to be worried about? What if it's those other two guys, and they follow me or go after Racheal and Starbright?

This day is going down as the worst ever. Point blank period. As I find my way to the door I remember. It leads to a service elevator, and you need a keycard to access that lift. From the staff closet, I find a clean uniform and quickly pull it on over my dress from last night, concealing it quite well under the frumpy fabric. I wish I could hide my face better, but there isn't anything that is part of this uniform that could do that without looking even more suspicious. Ironically, I have to show more of my face to blend in because the maids are required to wear their hair in a tight bun at the nape of the neck.

I grab a few tissues from a workstation and wipe my mouth clean of the lipstick I just put on. I don't want anyone to look at me at all. I want to be as plain as a girl named Jane. From the workstation, I spy a badge with a keycard, and I swipe it, feeling super guilty for stealing it, but I have no other choice right now. I'll figure out a way to make it right later on. If I survive this. Whatever this is.

Taking a deep breath, I try to slow down my heart as it thumps almost painfully in my chest, feeling stressed to the freaking max. The heavy metal door is loud as I try to pull it open, scraping against an ill-fitting frame from its age and use. Once open, I slowly peer out into the hallway and make sure everything is clear. All seems silent as the dead. One last deep breath, and I make a run for it, pushing a cart full of cleaners and laundry in front of me to continue with blending in.

I swipe the elevator with my keycard, and I'm right back to where I was this morning, begging God to open an elevator door. Except for this time, it falls much faster, and the door springs open without men trying to shoot my face off, much to my pleasure and grateful soul.

It doesn't take me long to remember my way around the building from this access point. Once the elevator lands on the right floor, I use my keycard on a new room, praying when I turn the handle no one will be on the other side.

The room is posh, and whoever is staying here is too. I quickly find a new outfit in the closet to change into, run from the room, and find my way back to the elevator. Inside the confinement of the metal walls, I use my lipstick from my bag to block out the watchful eye of the security camera.

Quickly I change my clothes from the horrible stuffy maids' uniform to the nice black dress that I took from that guest's room. I'll figure out how to make things right later. For now, I shake out my wash and go, and when the bell rings to the lobby floor, I try to not run as fast as possible to the door. Ditching the bundle of clothes in a trash can in the hall, I do my best to pace myself and look casual.

I try to use the side furthest from the counter, and my plan seems to work as I make my way to the door, finding freedom. It's a little chilly outside as I make my escape. I hug my arms around my body and slice through the thick lines of people that fill the sidewalk.

It only takes me a few minutes to get to the

campus, and when I do, I take a good look around, scanning the crowd to make sure I don't see any of the men, including Umberto, from the hotel where the shit went down earlier. All I see are guys my age dressed in hoodies staring at their phones while with a group of so-called friends.

I know I sound bitter, but really, my generation needs to do better. As a society, we definitely need to look up more, and down at our phones less. Hell, look at what just happened to me. What if I hadn't been paying attention? I might have been killed without even seeing the faces of my killers or shot in the crosshairs of their fight with Umberto. The thought sends a shiver down my spine.

Anyhow... I make my way back to my dorm room only to find that the sign on the damn door is flipped again, which is supposed to signal that my roomy is hooking up with someone and I cannot interrupt them. Which really pisses me off. I need to get into my room.

I storm myself to the cafe to check on Rachel. I also double-check to make sure I'm not being followed. Starbright is working today, and I ask her if she's seen Racheal, but she says she has the day off. I ask her if I can work because hell, at least I'll be around people here until my class begins. But she refuses, telling me some bullshit about how I need to align my chakras and shit. *Whatever, sis.*

So I make my way back to the dorms. The sign is still flipped on the door, and I don't even care this time. I bust my way in and gasp when I step through. On my bed is a sight I did not expect to find... never, never, never. And no, this isn't like that one time when I found my roomy having sex on the computer desk with mystery man number 300. This is like some crazy stalker type of thing.

It's him.

On my purple comforter-covered bed is Umberto Bova. I try to escape, but he rushes the door and grabs me around the waist, pulling me back into the room. His hand is gloved, and he covers my mouth for a second.

"I'm not here to hurt you," he says seriously, moving his hand away. "But I need you to listen."

"Get away from me!" I kick at him, but his lethal hands hold me still.

"You're gonna need me, Victoria. So, I suggest you listen to what I say, and do not try to fight me on this. Either way, pretty girl, you're coming with me. So, let's just make it easy on us both, got it?"

"Get the fuck away from me." I refrain from spitting at him. I'm too damn classy to be caught up in some Jerry Springer type of fight. Instead, I try to knee him in the balls, but he's too damn fast and dodges my attempt.

"I don't know why you're running from me, babe. I'm not your problem."

"But you damn sure ain't my solution."

"That's to be determined."

CHAPTER SEVEN

Victoria

Umberto takes my wrists and pins me to the wall. I'd love to say that it disgusts me, but secretly it turns me the hell on. Way on. I don't feel scared of him even though I know I should. There's just nothing in my body that feels like it's warning me to escape from him. No red alerts. Instead, all I want to do is get closer to him.

Did Starbright put some kind of hippy spell on me or something? What is this feeling I have right now? A man I hardly know is inside of my dorm room after shooting his way out of a hotel (I assume), and I am honest to God turned on by him, pinning me to the wall.

Being in this position makes me aware of a new fact; Umberto has a gun on him. I swallow hard, but he only watches the rise and fall of my chest as I take deep breaths. I want to crash my lips into his. I want him to shove me to my knees and demand to have his dick sucked by my lips.

Holy shit. I am going to hell, aren't I?

"I'm not the solution, huh?" he laughs darkly, whispering in my face. "I don't think you understand what's going on here. You need me."

"I don't need shit."

"That's where you're wrong, pretty girl. You need a lot of shit from me."

He challenges me, staring deep into my eyes with his raven-black irises. My clit aches at the threat of him entering my pussy with his huge cock again. I want him so badly I can still taste his kiss from last night.

I lean forward and gently nip at his plump bottom lip with my teeth, then lick my tongue across the spot I nipped to soothe the pain.

"See," Umberto moans before expertly ripping my borrowed dress in half. I'm going to be mad about that later, but right now, I just don't care. "You definitely me."

I moan as he roughly grasps my hair with his still gloved hands and crashes his lips onto mine.

I let him kiss me and even kiss him even more passionately in return, biting on his full bottom lip as I melt like putty in his hands. His fingers roam my mound to find the underside of my Victoria's Secret panties and push them aside so he can swipe a long digit across my soaked pussy lips. My legs fall open as I silently beg for more.

"Take the gloves off," I whisper.

"You really want to wait?"

Hell no, I don't want to wait. I want him to shove those thick gloved fingers up my cunt and make me come just like I crave. My wet pussy is practically begging for it as I gyrate my hips enticingly.

Umberto gazes deep into my eyes as he finger-fucks me hard, pumping at a feverish rate. I am so close to exploding around his hand. I cry out and moan and beg for more. Part of me wants to fucking laugh at how I am now the girl getting mine in this room after being kicked out so many damn times. My roomy could never top this. I'd like to see her try to get finger-fucked against the door after a gunfight, by a man that could easily hold me his prisoner. I think I just upped the game of this whole do not disturb if the 'fuck' sign is on.

"Do you remember how last night ended, baby?" he teases. "You drank too much and didn't get the chance to be properly fucked like I planned. I rather you be sober when I fuck you ten ways from Sunday."

"Screw you, Umberto."

He kisses me hard and then falls to his knees to eat my pussy like it's a delicious cupcake. His tongue flicks over my aching bud until my knees tremble like crazy, and my body begins to quiver and quake. Umberto slaps his fingers over my sex, punishing me blissfully.

"Do you always let strange men sneak into your dorm and make you come like this, Victoria? Do you like almost getting caught? What if your roommate were to walk in on us right now? What if she saw me eat your pussy like this?"

He licks me again, over my sensitive clit, and I moan loudly, my voice bouncing off the walls of the room.

Umberto kisses my thighs again before pulling away. He pulls his dick free from his pants as he rises to his feet. He's so damn big and thick; I have no idea how that monster dick will fit into my sore snatch today.

"Suck me, baby."

"Mmm, yes. I want it so bad."

"Show me, Victoria. Show me how bad you want this cock to make you come. I might just oblige."

I fall to my knees and bob on his dick like I'm working for the relief of orgasming because damn it, I am. I love the taste of him and how his thick cock hits the back of my tight throat. I suck him hard as I take him down my throat again and again, making him moan for me to let him come in my mouth.

I love how his fingers are twisted in my coils as I tease the tip of his swollen dick and take him deep until he's on the edge of coming down my throat. Umberto pulls away and quickly lifts me to my feet, spins me around, and presses me against the door.

"Your mouth is fucking magical," he growls in my ear. "And I know this pussy is too."

His dripping cock presses against my wet lips, and I cry out as he sinks slowly inside of me, claiming me as his. I start to rub my needful clit feverishly; wanting to come so damn bad as he pounds into me. I feel him stretch me with his thickness, while a delicious burn starts to build inside of me. Every sensation combined quickly sends me flying high above the clouds.

I can't help myself as I reach back to grab hold of his thick dark locks and shamelessly beg him to beat my pussy harder. He obliges my needs until we're coming together. The chorus of our moans filling up the tiny room as sex fills the air and sweat trickles down our bodies. I forget all about the weather outside and how cold I was less than an hour ago as I had rushed over to the cafe.

Damn it, the cafe. Racheal!

"Shit, get off me." I push at him, looking frantically around the room for my panties. He's lucky he's so damn good at making me come, or I would be really pissed off about that dress right now. How am I supposed to get it cleaned and returned to its owner now?

"I have to find Racheal," I say in a hurry, flying to my closet to find something else. I opt this time for something more suitable for the cold air outside, even though I'm still overheated from that amazing sex. I slip on a light pink pair of sweats and a matching top and jacket.

Umberto snickers as he tugs his pants back on, his hair a wild mess on top of his head from my roughness. Oops.

"What's so damn funny?" I ask.

"Nothing, it's just you look like cotton candy. In a good way. Like I'd love to rip that pink shit all off of you and eat that sweet pussy of yours all over again."

I try to form a coherent sentence.

"I need to find Racheal."

"Pretty girl, you're mine. Did you forget? Do you need a reminder?" He crosses the room and electricity walks with him, coursing its way right back between my legs.

"Pretty*boy*, I belong to no one. Not a damn soul. And my friend might be in danger, thanks to you and whoever those thugs were. I need to find her."

"No one gives a shit about her. You're the only one in danger, Victoria Holt, heiress to the Holt empire."

"I'm not an heiress to anything. If you knew me beyond the tabloids, then you would know that, smartypants."

"You're in danger standing right where you are because I'm in the same room as you. Because, as I said, you're mine."

"Look, Umberto, I know some girls love all this super possessive stuff, but I'm not one of them. I happen to be a very independent woman who speaks my mind and works for what I have. So, while it's very cute and all that you'd like to be my man, I'll have to pass on the offer. We've known each other for like—" I snap my fingers. "Two seconds."

He grins. "You're going to be fun, you know that?"

Umberto lets out a hard breath as he tucks his hands in his trouser pockets, revealing guns on each of his sides as he pushes back his suit jacket. My heart races. What the hell? Who needs that many guns on their body?

"I know we have shared our names, but I guess we have not been properly introduced yet, Victoria. I'm Umberto Bova, and I run New York. My biggest fans called me Lucifer as a compliment. And my enemies don't get a chance to make up names because, well..." he shrugs with a glint of sheer wickedness in his dark midnight eyes. "Maybe that's for another time. But my point is, no one in this city tells me no. Not the people who owe me money. Not the people who work for me and my crew. And not princesses who fuck like goddesses and have big plans to become a doctor. Now..." he glances down at the hammer on his weapon. "Once again, we can do this the hard way, or we can do this my way. I prefer my way. It ends with a lot more orgasms and a lot less shit to cover up."

I'm stunned into silence, which is not an easy feat. How did I get here? All I wanted was a cup of coffee, and now I'm being claimed. No wait...

kidnapped? Is that what the hell this is? And what is he going to do with me after that? Should I fight? Should I scream? Is he joking? He laughs again as he scans over my clothes.

"I'm not going–"

"Babe, it's already tough enough that you're gorgeous, but you're gonna have to lose the cotton candy outfit. Gangsters don't make themselves obvious, and you are a neon sign lighting up the sky in that thing. So like I said, are we doing this the hard way or the easy way?"

Well, damn.

I guess he is serious.

CHAPTER EIGHT

Victoria

There's a section of housing I've only heard about in New York. It's called Billionaires Row, and the only reason I know anything about any 'rows' belonging to billionaires is that I saw it on Bravo's Million Dollar Listing. That is as close as I ever got to seeing a property like that. How sad, right? A girl that grew up in the public eye with parents owning the better portion of hotel real estate doesn't even have a condo. Dammit, I don't even have a car.

After what happened with my parents's fortune,

I never thought in a million years I'd be anywhere near this type of luxury and exclusiveness. Not only do investors like experts of Wall Street type men live here, but also, the tech type of dudes, and then, of course, movie stars and athletes and people from those walks of life.

If you're somebody big in the world, you live here, basically. And apparently, you don't even have to make a legitimate living to be either. You can be a straight-up mafia gangster and have a condo worth millions of dollars in one of the best zip codes in all of New York. This is where Umberto Bova decided to take me when he kidnapped me. A freaking luxury pad twenty stories in the sky.

"You like?" he asks.

"It's all right," I lie nonchalantly.

I grew up living in nice hotels all over the world, but I can't lie, they never came close to comparing to this place. First of all, just to get to his floor requires fingerprint verification and armed guards. Sure, they don't look armed, but it's the way they greet him and act that lets me know it's all very much a big deal, and what is worse is how they look at me. Has Umberto ever even had a woman up to his place before? Because by the way they stare at me, trying to figure out what the hell is going on, I'd venture to say he has not.

I know he must've had plenty of women with his body and sexual expertise, but I doubt he's ever had love or anything close. He doesn't exactly come off as the type who would partner up with a soulmate and let down his guard and share all his dirty little secrets. As much as I don't want to know any of this crap, I think I better start to pretend to care if I'm going to survive whatever the hell he has planned for me.

He said back at my dorm room that he thought I was an heiress to the Holt Hotel throne, but that's not in my future, despite what the press likes to report. They think my dad might be lying. As if he's got a secret stash of money or stocks somewhere. Trust me when I say he doesn't. I'm really just a big nobody these days. A college girl paying for my life with loans and as a job as a barista in a halfway decent coffee shop. My biggest claim to fame these days is making a killer macchiato.

Dammit, my stomach growls just thinking about sipping on that creamy deliciousness. I am so freaking hungry I could eat a dead rhino. Baha! What is wrong with me? Must be the lack of carbs.

I'm literally going insane. No carbs plus stressful mafia man encounter does not equal a healthy brain.

Umberto looks over at me as we ride the elevator up to his floor. The car has clear walls and gives us a view of the skyline as we are pulled up to the heavens. I feel like little Charlie from Willy Wonka in that scene where Wonka gives the boy the chocolate factory. This is just magical. Until my stomach growls again.

Just the thought of chocolate makes my mouth water. If I close my eyes, I can actually taste a Hershey bar. I've gotta stop this madness. My stomach growls again, and he turns to me, lifting his thick brows.

My God Umberto is a beautiful man. Everything about him is thick—and in all the right places. Shit. Now I'm feeling hungry in a much different sort of way.

"Are you hungry, Victoria?"

With a roll of my eyes, I tell him, "I've been hungry for weeks. Practically dreaming about food. I'd kill to be little Charlie from the Willy Wonka movie, right now."

He laughs, looking a bit surprised. "Why are you not allowing yourself to eat? You work at a cafe."

"Oh, I'm eating, but it's just that this diet I'm on

says I have to eat healthy foods, and I'm not very good at that. I grew up on room service."

"Tell me more."

"Like every morning, I'd start my day before school with a stack of blueberry pancakes covered in maple syrup, cheddar cheese omelets, and a big glass of chocolate milk. Either that or crepes with whipped cream and strawberries, or croissants with peaches and cream cheese, or french toast banana foster, with real vanilla bean ice cream melting on the side. Can't you tell? These hips and thighs don't lie."

The side of his mouth pulls tight. "You are so damn cute and sexy; you know that, right? Those delicious hips and thighs of yours could kill a man."

"I'm hungry. That's what I am," I huff and blush at the same time.

He smiles, looking at the door when it dings and spreads wide open. But there is another door, and he has to use a key to enter. That door slides into the wall, revealing the inside of his luxury condo. And daaaaaamn. It is posh. I don't even want to step inside.

Everything is gleaming and pearly white and smells incredible. The intoxicating scent of leather and flowers swirls inside the large space. Most New

Yorkers don't even get an eighth of what he has in square footage. Umberto owns basically twenty apartments. That's how many you could easily fit into this place. Not to mention the outdoor patio that has a glass ceiling and gives the most amazing view of the city, like you're just flying above everyone else, and they could never reach your level, figuratively or literally.

"I'll get a reservation at a nice place. You'll eat."

I laugh at him. "I'm not exactly dressed to go out to dinner." I changed from my cotton candy pink sweats into my all black sweats. It's called compromise. Plus, it's laundry day; there wasn't much else to choose from. "One doesn't know what to wear for a kidnapping."

"Is that what you think this is?"

"Isn't it?"

"How you're dressed is no problem. I'll make arrangements for that as well. I need to get to work. You can play while I'm out." He sounds so damn sure of himself.

"This isn't a game to me, Umberto. I have a life. I have school and work and friends. I have a job I need to show up at, so I can pay rent and bills and feed myself. I live in the real world where people expect to be paid with money that gets taxed, not this scheming lifestyle you live by."

"I make money that is taxed, too." He says it with a grin, and honestly, I don't want to know how or why. I doubt he'd tell me anyhow. "Come."

He shows me a few of the rooms and the common areas like bathrooms and kitchen and stuff. He even shows me how to work the huge TV, but the thing has so many buttons, I don't think I'll even try. Plus, he has quite the collection of books, and honestly that's more my speed unless there's a crappy reality TV show because that's the one vice I can't shake and do allow myself to enjoy fully.

"This is your room," he says, pushing open a door at the end of a long hallway. The space is of course, just as beautiful as the rest of the condo and about ten times bigger than my dorm room. I could fit ten dorms plus the coffee shop in this place. Not too many people can say that about a bedroom in the city.

"Who usually sleeps here?" I ask suspiciously.

"No one. I'm rich. I just have the extra rooms because I can."

"You're so arrogant. Money doesn't last forever."

"Mine will."

I walk slowly around the perimeter of the room.

Everything is pristine and decorated in sleek black and white colors with pops of silver and gold. The bed is dressed in a fluffy white downy blanket that mimics a cloud. It looks so damn comfy. As I look at it, I realize I'm beyond tired, but my stomach is still groaning in hunger.

"I'll make that reservation." Umberto takes a step back, pulling out his cellphone. "In the meantime, I'll have the maid bring you some snacks."

Before he can walk away, I turn to him. "This is really nice and all, but I think you have misunderstood what a one night stand is. It literally means we fuck each other one night. Not move in together."

He chuckles sinisterly. "We fucked twice and you're a brat."

"Can this *brat* leave?"

"Why would you want to? You can't even sleep in your own dorm room when you want. Here you've got carte blanc access to the entire house"

"Can. I. Go."

Umberto rolls his eyes, ignoring me, and starts to scroll through some sort of list on his phone.

"Seriously though. Why exactly do you want me here with you, Umberto? You can have any woman you want. I'm just a broke college kid. This makes no sense at all."

Umberto's brows pull tight for a moment. He clears his throat, punches something on his phone, and then speaks in beautiful Italian so smoothly to someone on the other end. All Umberto offers me is a whispered, "I'll see you at dinner." Before he disappears from my sight.

In a matter of hours, I am groomed and treated to all kinds of wonderfulness as woman after woman comes up to my room offering me hairstyling, a manicure, a pedicure, the most amazing makeup, clothes, and even a freaking massage. This is beyond anything that I expected. Even my parents never treated themselves to these kinds of perks.

I shouldn't accept any of this though. It's clear this man is not a good man. He confessed to basically being a criminal, and for all I know, getting mixed up with him like this could make me just as guilty as him. It's not what I planned on when I hooked up with him, that's for sure. And it definitely is not what I think of when someone is kidnapping you. I guess it could be worse. I could be tied up in a dungeon or some crap. I don't even know why he'd want me though. I keep replaying the last 24 hours over in my head, and none of it makes any sense.

After my pampering crew leaves and I am smelling, looking and feeling damn good, I dig through my purse for my cell, but it's gone. I look around for another phone to use in the condo, but there isn't anything here either. I head to the elevator and press the button, but it won't unlock without Umberto's key. I scream and curse at him. I am literally trapped here. What if a damn fire broke out?

Motherfucker.

I am so mad. I might be pretty and free of knots in my shoulders and back, but still, so damn mad at Umberto Bova. Who does he think he is?

I go back to my room and plop down on the bed, not giving a damn anymore about keeping my makeover intact because I don't care. If I'm a mess, then that serves him right for forcing me to be here.

A person at their worst doesn't deserve to have me at my best.

CHAPTER NINE

Umberto

A m I on drugs? I've locked up Victoria Holt inside of my fucking fortress as if it was a good idea. I am straight up losing my mind these days. What is this girl doing to me? It's like her smile, that laugh, her quick wit, and let's be real– that pussy has some magical epic force over my brain cells. I need to send an SOS or some shit to be rescued from whatever the hell this is.

I am *not* this kind of guy, and I'm not talking about the guy who kidnaps motherfuckers. I am *totally* that fucking guy. I'm talking about the guy who mixes business with pleasure. The guy who is willing to put all his shit on the line for a hot piece of perfect ass and pussy. I'm not that guy.

The real problem though, is that it's more than that. She fucking does something to my chest that makes it hurt. Like the thought of her walking out of my life and me not having her fucking hurts. And to make matters worse, I have *actual* fucking problems that need to be dealt with like yesterday. One of them being that Dema is still breathing.

He needed a bullet in his fucking brain a week ago. I'm about to become a joke and lose serious clout in the family because I am spiraling out of control thanks to a girl named Victoria Holt.

Speaking of her... I looked into her background. I know who she is. This girl is on some other level of a *gangster* in my opinion because she is actually trying to play it off like she's some normal chick who attends college and makes lattes for a living and that's it. When in actuality, she is the motherfucking Bonnie to my Clyde, even if she is broke. Her fucking parents never bothered to set up a trust fund for her, so when they went broke, so did she.

She's big time, deserves the best, and I'm about to make her remember it. But first, I have to deal with the issue of her deadbeat daddy as well as keeping

her around and making her see that I can actually
help her.

So yeah, I fucking brought her to my actual
home, where I sleep and eat and do normal fucking
things. Mostly. So why do it? Well, for starters, my
home has every comfort she could desire. Egyptian
cotton sheets dress every bed along with a bounty of
goose-down filled pillows and blankets so thick and
fucking heaven-like you'd never want to wake up.
There are flat screen tv's in every room and a
gourmet kitchen made for a professional chef. I can
afford all of this and more because I run my own
family under the umbrella of the Andolini
Syndicate. I own this fucking city and I make the
rules.

I leave Victoria to all that comfort so I can deal
with the bullshit of Dema at the titty bar I handle all
my affairs from. I never do fucking work at home.
That is a rule I will never break. It could be bugged,
or the FEDS could raid it at any moment, and I don't
like surprises.

At home you get comfy. You forget things. You
leave things open you don't think about. Work is just
that. A fucking place to run shit. I am on my game
here. I don't take chances with my money, name, or
freedom. Every day I park my car behind the

building and hand the keys over to a goon I call TipToe. He's built like a linebacker, and no one would dare try to touch me with him out there.

This joint is one of the best in the city, but I'm not the sole owner. I am just a silent partner that funnels my shit through this club in order to stay clean and free of trouble from my friends in the government. I do, however, take the competition seriously, and there is some major fucking competition for tits and ass in my town. I refuse to be last in anything, just on principle. They can suck my dick and try to take my spot as boss of this city, but they'll never beat me.

Most of the families in mafia organizations own titty bars. It's not a new idea. But my girls are the best you'll find. Best tit jobs. Best faces. Best pussy. But that's not really the hub of this place—I've got bigger dreams than that. No, I use this place as a hub for my deals. Titty bars are a cash business, and that's very important when ninety-nine percent of your income doesn't come from legal gains. This is my one percent. And there's no way for the FEDS to track the other ninety-nine. That's the way I like it. And it's a much better cover-up.

As soon as I enter the club I am hit by the aroma of perfume and hairspray and whatever else the girls use to look like supermodels and earn almost as much as the real thing in a night's work for toying with helpless fools that can't get pussy this good at home, or fucking at all.

"Hello, Mr. Bova."

"Evening, Mr. Bova."

They all stare and greet me as I slice my way through the darkened room. The truth is, the people in this city all want to be me as I make my way toward the back where the real business is conducted. The men that is. The women just want to be *with* me. Fuck me. Have me spend my money and power on them. Spill it across their big bouncy fake tits like a bottle of champagne. But I don't drink the cheap bottles. And I don't stick around for cuddling after a good fuck.

Love sure as hell isn't on my radar, let alone the girlfriend thing. So why the fuck do I keep thinking about Victoria Holt as I walk by all of these beautiful women? She's just a college kid. The daughter of a deadbeat. She should be out of my system by now.

Yet, she isn't.

"Capo," Karlita, greets me as she enters my office and closes the door.

I waste no time getting down to business. "Everything in order for tonight?"

"S*i*, sir. We are scheduled to go as planned."

"Did Victoria get pampered at the house?"

"S*i*."

"And she didn't refuse anything?"

"No, sir."

"Good. You have my car ready?"

"S*i*, Mr. Bova."

"And the care-package?"

"It's on your desk."

I glance at a yellow envelope and nod. That is the newest info on where that fuck Dema has been hiding out. I have spies all over the city. He has nowhere to fucking run. Honestly, it's beneath me that I even have to do this but my hitman fucked up which means now I have to handle it myself. It's the only way I know things will get done.

"Do me a favor. Make sure I'm not disturbed. I want to get out of here early tonight."

"Will do."

Karlita nods her pretty little head of curly red hair. Such a stark contrast to Victoria. Victoria Holt is a fine twist of curves and hills with a little extra meat in all the right places. Her curls are dark. Her tits are full and round. And she always smells like a hint of vanilla and cinnamon. Her pussy tastes like it too.

I can't wait to wrap my lips around her buttery soft tits again. I want to taste her so badly I can hardly keep myself from growling at the thought of tracing my tongue across her warm skin.

After my meeting with Karlita, I dig deeper into Victoria's past before I decide to make my way back to the condo. I just have to make a quick stop along the way and handle some business.

CHAPTER TEN

Victoria

"Yes. Grow, baby, grow. Get bigger, you sexy little things. Rise high and big. I can't wait to stuff your sweetness into my mouth and swallow you whole."

My mouth waters as I think about swallowing these damn blueberry muffins whole.

I've been whipping up food ever since I got over pouting about being locked in here.

I figured I was locked away in a glamorous ass house stocked full of all kinds of organic foods and bomb ass baking tools and plenty of kitchen counter space, so I might as well take advantage.

Plus, I wonder if this was a secret lesson from God, hidden in plain sight, to not ever ignore my stomach when it's growling out in need of some damn yummy tasting scrumptiousness.

Screw fasting.

I am living to eat this food tonight. It looks like someone with the damn munchies broke in Umberto's house, not gonna lie. I'm not a smoker, but I love me some snacks. I basically live for them. I don't know why I have been denying myself all these weeks, and once I started baking, I made everything I've been craving for weeks.

In addition to the muffins, I make dutch apple pie, cupcakes with homemade cream cheese frosting, pancakes with chocolate chips, spaghetti and meatballs made from scratch, some grilled cheese sandwiches with some fancy-ass cheese he had in his fridge, and lastly, I make homemade mac-n-cheese with an even fancier type of cheese, plus regular cheddar (because come on now; you don't go messing with mac-n-cheese like that. It's a classic).

I take a look around the gourmet kitchen and kind of laugh to myself because the place looks like a restaurant, not someone's personal home kitchen. I do love cooking. I loved it as a kid too. I was always sneaking into the hotel kitchens of whatever place we were at and watching as the kitchen crew created all kinds of dishes and gourmet cuisine. Depending on where we were, it was a new experience most of the time. And the best part was that I could try whatever I wanted, on the house. And of course, however much I wanted.

So, there were mornings I woke up to stacks of crepes or eggs Benedict and then nights where I tucked into warm chocolate chip cookies or Bavarian cream-filled donuts.

For my birthdays, I celebrated with towering cakes that had sparklers dazzling on top of the highest tier, or with cakes that were huge stacks of donuts drizzled in icing and rainbow sprinkles. That, of course, was when the kitchen staff was in charge of my food. When my parents were in charge, you know when they actually remembered they had a daughter, it was more like the fancy stuff. Lobster and filet mignon. Duck confit with beet soup and cauliflower puree and other weird stuff I turned my nose up at, but their adult guests revered.

I glance back at my muffins; they are sky high and cracked down the middle just like they should be, signaling they are done to perfection. I pull my tray out of the oven and settle it down on the cooling rack. The smell is to die for. I imagine this is what Heaven smells like—vanilla, berries, and Italian food cooking in the background. That's my kind of Heaven, anyhow.

After quickly unloading the tray of muffins, I turn around to stick it in the sink, when I'm suddenly scared stupid by the ghost of Umberto Bova in the doorway. How the hell did I not hear him come up?

He stands there like a damn statue watching me, not saying a single word as he toys with his keys as if he's not sure what the hell to do with himself. Well, haha, that makes two of us, Umberto Fucking Bova. I'm kind of a prisoner trapped here, so calm your tits and don't get pissed that I want to occupy myself by way of delicious home-cooked food.

"Don't stand there staring like you didn't know I was stuck here while you went around doing whatever dangerous gangster stuff you were out there doing. I'm stuck here without anything to keep me busy or anyone to give me company, except for the comfort of the food network. Thankfully your staff knows how to stock this kitchen properly. You're out of milk, by the way. I'm sure you have someone appointed as your own personal organic milk fetcher who probably has to go to a dairy farm and milk the cow themselves just to be sure you get the very best available, so you might want to let them know."

Umberto raises a brow. I raise mine right back. "Oh, I'm sorry. Am I supposed to be scared of you and your menacing brows or something? Sorry to disappoint you, Umberto Bova... " I reach out and grab hold of a warm muffin, ripping a hefty bite away with my teeth as I start to feel myself become overwhelmed by everything coming out of my mouth. Best to stuff it, right? Wrong. I talk around the muffin because apparently word vomit is on the menu tonight. "...but I have been hurt by people much worse than you. You'd have to get on my parent's level if you want to really dig your proverbial heels in and try to damage my heart any further. Because I am pretty damn hurt already."

I start to cry and toss the muffin near his head when he dodges it and grins at me.

"Glad I can entertain you," I say.

He shakes his head and steps closer. And I wish I felt like I could hate him somehow, but I just don't. I actually want him to come to me like I'm a magnet, and my whole body just pulls him in to connect.

Umberto brushes my hair away from my face, and if I were stupid, I'd swear he actually looked concerned, but smart girls know that bad boys like him who kidnap innocent people and lock them up don't give two hot damns about being kind or someone else's feelings. Still, his eyes make a liar out of both him and myself because they grow deeper and softer as he stares at me. And then he smiles, and he seems pretty darn amused rather than offended or pissed off that I basically just mouthed off to him for three minutes straight.

"What?" I bark at him.

He grins like the sly man that he is. "You did all of this?"

"Well, it damn sure wasn't Emeril Lagasse."

"Where did you learn to cook?"

"Do you really care?"

"Actually, I do. I take my food very seriously. I even own a few five-star restaurants to prove it."

"Yeah," I chuckle, "I'm *sure* that's what those places are for."

"What's that supposed to mean?" He asks in a serious manner, but the laughter in his eyes gives him away. He already knows what I'm implying. I answer him anyway just to humor him and myself.

"I know that Italian mobsters use restaurants to front your real-real business ventures."

"Is that so." He grins, picking up a cupcake. He

licks the top ring of icing off, and I have never seen anything sexier in my entire life.

"Of course it is." I swallow hard. "I know all about you guys."

"How's that? Do you make a habit of having one night stands with... men in the same profession as me?"

"I've watched enough Netflix docu-series and Scarface movies to know how it all works, boo. It doesn't exactly take a genius to figure it all out."

"Ah, but you are a bit of a smartypants, aren't you? Ranked at the top of your class. Favorited by the dean and by your professors. Right, future Doctor Holt?"

I cock my head to the side. "How do you know that?"

"I know a lot about you."

"I gathered that, Umberto," I huff. "But how? What are you spying on me? Have you been watching me? Tell me, was any of this organic? Did any of it happen naturally? Did we meet by accident in that cafe? Or has this all just been some elaborate scheme of yours all along? God, you must feel so damn proud, huh? Tricking me like this? Getting your way? You must think I'm a damn fool, right? Ain't that right?"

Umberto softens, putting the cupcake down, and then props my chin on his fingertips. I want to pull away. I should pull away from him. It would be the smart thing to do. He has admitted to being dangerous. He has kidnapped me. He has kept me here against my will (I think), and now he's telling me he knows things about me that I have never told him about myself, which only means something bad. He's checked on me. He's found out things. But how and more importantly – why?

I shiver a bit, and he looks me over, his heavy dark brows pinching in the middle of his forehead. He has a prominent vein that reveals itself when he looks worried, like a little lightning bolt flashing across the tanned skin of his forehead, playing peek-a-boo.

Against my better judgment, I reach up and brush my finger across it. He gasps a little, and it sends my heart into a tailspin. I don't even know why. There is just something that lives between us that I can't control. And by the looks of him, breathing heavier and coming closer to my mouth, it would seem like he feels the same exact way.

"I think you're a goddess," he says softly. "I think you're the most beautiful fucking thing I have ever laid my eyes on."

I gasp. My stomach flip-flops, and it's not because of the sudden influx of carbs. My heart flutters like the wings of a hummingbird, faster than it has ever beaten in my chest before. It feels like it's going to fly away before I can even catch my breath.

"What are you saying? Why do you do this to me? How can you make me feel like this? I barely even know you?"

"Some things are just destiny, Victoria. Some things are beyond common sense explanations."

His words pierce my heart. "Destiny," I mumble. "That's what she named me."

Umberto grins all sexily. "She must've had a feeling about you. By the way, I had someone check on your friend too. She's fine."

"Good, that makes me feel a little better, but why are you keeping me here? Why are you doing this if you feel this way about me? Kidnapping me is not going to help you get on my good side."

Umberto brushes his rough fingers along my flushed cheek, sending a firestorm into the pit of my stomach. "You have to trust me, Victoria."

"That's not easy to do."

"I know, but you have to try. Just like I have to try to handle you being here. That is not easy for me, either."

"Then let me go."

"No," he roars. "You're mine and you're staying right fucking here where I can protect you."

"Don't you think I should have a choice?"

His brows pinch together again, the lightning bolt vein revealing itself once more. He's frustrated with my unwillingness to be here. Almost as if he's biting back what he really wants to say.

"Umberto, please just tell me *why* I am here. The real reason."

But before he can answer, he doubles-over, holding his hand across his stomach.

"Oh my God. Umberto! What's wrong?"

"I was hurt earlier. It's not a big deal, really."

He hobbles off to the bathroom, and I stupidly follow. I watch as he strips out of his jacket and tosses it like it isn't one of the most expensive pieces of fabric in the world, on the floor. Then he rips open his black button-down, and I gasp loudly at the scene underneath. Umberto is covered in blood across his ripped torso.

"What happened to you?!" I demand to know.

Umberto laughs at my question. Freaking laughs! I huff at him as I rush to his side to help him out, but he puts out a hand to keep me away.

"I'm a big boy. I can do it myself, Victoria."

"Yeah, well, I'm two years into becoming a doctor, so I'd wager that makes me more qualified than you, Mr. Strip club and Restaurant owner slash gangster."

"How about not repeating that last part again," he seethes.

"Why? Will you kill me if I do?"

"I'd never hurt a fly." Okay, that sounded more than a little sarcastic coming from him.

"Just park your buns made of steel over on that expensive ass tub of yours and let me do my thing."

He grins at me. "I do like it when you're bossy."

"I am not bossy. I am just a woman who knows what the hell I am doing, and you're obviously a fool because you went out and got yourself into a mess like this. What kind of fool gets... what is this? Were you cut by a knife? Damn it, Umberto, you should have gone to a hospital. What were you even thinking?"

"Worried about me dying, love?"

I huff at him. "I am worried about being left here locked up in this princess tower like your little pet, for one. And two, yes, I don't want to see you die any more than I want to see anything else hurt.

"That's some sweet shit, Victoria." He practically rolls his sexy dark eyes at me. "I feel so honored."

"Don't get too high on that horse there. I have a soft spot for all living creatures. I don't want to see you hurt any more than I want to see a dog or like a cockroach or a snake hurt. If you get what I'm saying."

"Yeah, yeah," he chuckles. "I'm picking up what you're throwing down, pretty girl. You think I'm a snake. A vile little thing. Well, baby, guess what? Snakes can also be beneficial to the ecosystem. They get rid of undesirables."

"Justify yourself however you like, just let me clean your wound before it gets infected while you do it."

He shrugs. "Suit yourself, love."

I get to work on him. I've read dozens of texts about what to do as part of my education, but I've never actually put those words into action. I feel completely unready for this type of thing. It is not that I am nervous about the actual work itself, I mean a child could clean and dress a wound like this, but I'm nervous to be so close to him.

This isn't sexual. There's no alcohol or lust involved. This is just me having to touch him with care and consideration. And then of course I'm also nervous that he was to watch me as I tend to him under this setting.

I have to not care about him and therein lies the problem. I do care about him. I am actually worried about the man who probably almost got me shot in the hotel. The man who has now kidnapped me. I should be glad that he is hurt. I should be glad that he is in pain. But I am not.

I do not find a single ounce of joy in his pain or in the thought of someone cutting him with a sharp object. Although, I do have to wonder what kind of situation he got himself involved in to warrant another person wanting to harm in such a demented manner.

Even as a woman held here against my will, I still do not wish to harm him. In fact, it is quite the opposite. I want him to be okay. I want to see him smile. Ugh, is this my 'daddy issues' showing? Shit. I am not going to even think about that. There aren't enough carbs or sugary sweets in all of New York to handle that kind of mind fuckery right now.

I sigh hard. And then I get to work.

A warm wet washcloth lets me clean the mess of blood off his chest pretty well, and like most injuries such as this, once the blood is gone, the actual wound isn't so bad. He just got hit in an unfortunate place that makes it look way worse than it actually is.

As a kid, I got hit in the head once when I was

climbing the wrong way up a slide. I foolishly didn't do two things. One, I didn't listen when my sitter told me not to do that. Two, I didn't see a huge plank of wood that was right in my path, and my head headed straight for it with the force of what felt like a freaking freight train speeding through the night. My poor head busted open like a damn, sending a river of blood streaming down my face and across my pretty white dress.

I can laugh about it now, but it was a scene from a horror movie, to be honest. Mothers screamed and swept up their little ones in a mad rush to flee from the playground. My poor nanny went as white as a ghost before fainting at the sight of all the blood. I had to walk myself over to the bathroom and figure it all out.

Once I got my bleeding to stop, I cleaned the gash on my head and then used my headband and a lot of paper towels as a bandage. There wasn't much I could do about my poor white dress that was more red than a crispy bright white. It was scary, but it was also a bit empowering.

All of these so-called adults could not handle what I could, and I was only ten. It was like pulling back the curtain on a show about grown-ups and seeing what trickery went on behind the scenes. It was a real eye-opener, that's for sure. It also taught me that I wasn't afraid to be brave, or take care of myself without help, no matter how terrifying the situation presented itself. It gave me grit. It gave me balls. But it also made me feel incredibly alone.

Maybe that's why I am so drawn to Umberto. Sure, he chose this life for himself, but he still must be incredibly lonely living this way. On the outside, it all seems very posh and dreamlike, but imagine if you had to walk around constantly watching your back to make sure someone wasn't trying to stab you with a knife or shoot you with a gun. How horrifying.

He's a man with the whole weight of the world on his shoulders and no one to talk to about it with because who the hell could he possibly share such secrets with? Is that why he picked me? Does he think he can trust me with his darkest secrets?

It has to suck to not be able to talk about things. I know kind of how that feels. I have had to hide my history from almost every friend or wanna-be boyfriend I have ever had because I could never trust anyone was not using me for my money or social circle. Even as a kid. I never really had true friends. I had the people my mother wanted to network with in order to grow her empire. That worked out just lovely, by the way.

Not.

I have one friend with a fake name that is basically my friend by default, seeing as how we are scheduled and paid to be friendly to each other at the coffee shop. Not that Racheal isn't a nice girl, but I'm just saying. I don't trust people because of my past and my parents. Hell, I can't even trust them.

And I don't want to trust Umberto either, but I'm stuck here, and I feel like I'm going to have to make a move to try, or at least get to know him a little better if I have any chance of getting out of this somewhat unscathed. I truly believe if I tried to walk out of this gilded cage on my own that something would happen to me. I just don't know if it would be by him or someone other than him out there.

I take a deep breath and reach for some alcohol.

"That shit is gonna sting," he argues before I even get to dab it on the cotton swab. "Use something else."

"It could get infected. I guarantee you that scraping infected dead skin and muscle out of your body will hurt a lot more than a little swab of this, Bova."

"You think this is the first time I've ever had a

knife taken to me? Look at me, really look." He swings around and shows me faint scars buried under the dark ink on his chest and then his arms and hands.

"What the hell...what happened to you?"

"Life," he snickers. "Fucking life. I'm a fighter. That's all I know. I keep myself alive, and the only way to do that is to fight."

"Who the hell taught you that?"

He shrugs. "Hey, pass me what's in that drawer behind you."

I tug open the dark wood of the vanity drawer to find a bottle of scotch. "This?" I lift out the bottle and wave it at him.

"Fuck yes. Give that me, please."

"You really should not drink. Drinking only makes the healing process so much harder on your body."

He twists the cap off and takes a long swig directly from the bottle. "Good to know, babe." He goes back for a second and third swig. "Fuck, I needed something to just take the edge off."

"That's what you call taking the edge off, Umberto?"

"It's a very steep edge," he jokes. "You want some?" He offers me the bottle, but I shake my head.

"What's the matter? Think I'll try to take advantage of you? Think I'm that bad of a guy?"

"Just a heads up, you already have taken advantage of me, but yeah I think it's best if I just keep my wits about me in this situation."

"Baby, who took advantage of who? If you were so worried about that, you would have never let me touch you in the first place. I told you that night, in the cafe, when you were all snuggled up close to me on the sofa, I'm a dangerous man, don't fuck with me. What do you do? You flirt with me. You get in my car. You let me take you and eat that pussy and put my fingers in you until you came. It's a little late for trying to keep some sense about all this, don't you think?"

I scoff before quickly dousing him in a long squirt of alcohol and not the kind he likes drinking.

"Motherfucker!" He jumps, and I point at him.

"Do not disrespect me like that, Umberto. I don't give a rat's left nut sack who you think you are."

He chuckles darkly. "Oh baby, I love a feisty girl. Give me your best, I promise it is nothing compared to what I have seen or suffered before you, but damn it, I love that you have the balls to try, love. "

"Sit down and shut up. I have to dress your wound."

"I have a much better idea, Victoria. I could *un*dress you. We could have a lot of fun. Way more fun than this shit show, that's for damn sure. I could eat that sweet pussy all night long. You love it when I do that. I can tell it hasn't been done well before me. You have no idea how sweet and delicious you are."

My pussy clenches with muscle memory of all of the absolute truth he just spat. His tongue is a magical thing.

"The only thing getting eaten tonight are the cupcakes in the kitchen. Stuff your mouth with one of those, lover boy."

I toss band-aids at him and leave the bathroom before I do something stupid. Even more stupid than what got me here in the first place. I do not want to hook up with him. Not again.

Okay...maybe that's a damn lie.

CHAPTER ELEVEN

Victoria

If my poor neglected vagina could talk, she'd tell you that in our minds we have already fucked Umberto in the huge spa tub and on every flat surface in this house (and there is a fuck ton of square footage when it comes to counter space in this condo).

He is sinfully hot and I am drawn to him in a lethal way that should be against the law. He can't know that though. I hope I'm pulling off my whole "disinterested" thing, because in actuality I want to spread my legs for him every time I lay eyes on him.

I tell myself that carbs will erase the feelings of desire I have for Umberto Bova. I trot myself straight into the kitchen and whip up a big bowl of noodles and sauce and pile a dessert plate with a little bit of everything.

He has some big fancy-ass cappuccino maker in the kitchen that I want to get my hands on too, but honestly, that feels too much like slapping on my apron and calling myself Destiny. I don't want to be Destiny tonight. I want to be the girl who is watching Netflix and feeding my face until I am disgustingly full. Ridding myself of lustful thoughts.

Umberto has other plans, however. He comes out to the living room, changed into new clothes. He has a much more casual look of jeans and a tight-fitting white cotton shirt that shows every ounce of muscle in his well-defined arms. He has ink tattooed on his forearms and even on some of his fingers.

He sits down next to me and reaches for a cupcake but pauses when he glances over and sees me slurping noodles unabashedly beside him on the white sofa. At first, I think he's gonna give me shit for eating red sauce on his white furniture, but he cocks a brow at me and licks his lips.

"You made that?" he asks.

"I sure did." I shove a big bite in my mouth. "Mmm, so good."

"You can cook Italian food?"

"I can cook anything. I spent my childhood chasing chefs from all over the world around." I roll my eyes at him. "But you probably already know that since you have been spying on me and stuff."

"I didn't actually." He rubs his forehead and watches me devour my food. And then he laughs. "You're such a mystery to me, Victoria Holt. Even with all the info I have about you; you're nothing like what I keep expecting to find."

"What exactly do you know?"

He sighs a little. "Share with me a bite of your pasta, and I might feel inclined to share, too."

"Lean in close," I warn him. "Don't want to ruin whatever animal hide this expensive ass couch is made out of."

"It's not an animal, number one. And number two, if you stain the couch I'll just buy another one. I don't give a fuck about material things. Eh, for the most part."

He leans in as I twirl a forkful of pasta to feed him carefully. Watching him wrap his succulent lips around the noodles. It's like food porn.

"Then why have such a fancy home? And on Billionaire's row of all places?" I start to laugh, but he does not.

Umberto chews thoughtfully as he stares at me.

His tongue darting around his lips. "You honestly cooked that food? No lies?"

"Want more?" I grin.

"I want the whole fucking bowl, pretty girl. Pass it over."

"Nope. We had a deal, mister."

He sighs hard. "Fine. Okay. Jesus. Let's just say there's someone in your circle that owes me a debt, and I'm not a very nice guy when I'm not paid on time."

I shrug my shoulders. "What does that have to do with me? And I don't have a circle, so that can't even be true. I literally go to school and work, and there is no in-between. I'm a med student. We don't get to have lives or circles. We don't even get to sleep or eat."

"My sources say differently."

"Then you need to find new ones because they are wrong."

"Yeah?" He challenges. "So you don't know a guy named Dema Holt?"

Hearing him say my father's name jumpstarts my heart like I just got hit by a lightning bolt. My face must say it all.

Umberto grins a little. "Yeah, I thought so."

"How do you know my father?"

"The real question is how do I not know him. He owes practically everyone in New York something."

Umberto curls his finger at me, silently asking for another bite for him to keep talking. I blink rapidly out of my daze and oblige, feeding him a big twirl of spaghetti.

He chews carefully and then says, "I don't like handing out loans without insurance, but sometimes I am willing to take that chance based on what I need in return."

"What did you want my father to do for you?"

"That's not a question I'm going to answer regardless of how fucking incredibly good your cooking is. Next."

"Uh, thank you? And you still haven't explained what the hell I have to do with any of this. If you did your homework like you should have, you would know that I don't even talk to my father. I haven't talked to him in years."

"I know that now. Still, it doesn't change anything."

"It changes everything. Do you think he'll care that you have me here?"

"Yes."

I scoff. "I have news for you, Umberto Bova. My father hasn't given a damn a single day in his life about me. So you're going about getting whatever he owes you back in a very stupid way."

"Don't get angry with me, Victoria. Sometimes things start one way and then end up on a route you never even planned. Sometimes a change in plans is good."

"Good? I don't call being trapped with a criminal, with a damn gangster good, Umberto."

"Is that really all you think I am?" he asks, staring deeply at me with his dark eyes.

My heart stutters as I feel a stab of pain when he looks pained by my silence. I open my mouth to speak but can't find the words. Umberto groans a little.

"Do you remember the nice gentlemen who got off the elevator after our night together?"

I block out everything he brings to the surface when he mentions the night we had the most amazing sex of my entire life. Ugh. "No, I completely forgot." I roll my eyes. "Of course I remember. I'm not you. I don't get shot at every day of my life or threatened to be stabbed. Well, maybe in the fall when we run out of pumpkin spice syrup for our signature lattes, but bitches take their caffeine and seasons of weather very seriously these days."

His mood quickly changes as he laughs hard and

naturally, and it honestly warms me. I love that sound and feeling coming out of him. I love that I'm the reason for that sound. Umberto, on the other hand, looks as if he is embarrassed about it.

He probably doesn't do that often, I imagine. Laugh. I mean, how could he? He doesn't exactly live in a world full of comedians and humor or even humorous situations. I don't imagine threatening lives or stealing shit comes with many jokes.

He grows more serious and picks at the top of another cupcake, peeling away the icing.

"Those men don't take insurance policies, Victoria, and they damn sure don't take well to being ripped off."

"Are you saying that I was their target?"

His stare turns severe. "Well they damn sure weren't coming for *me*, love."

CHAPTER TWELVE

Victoria

"Are... are they still trying to kill me? Is that what they want to do?"

"You're safe here," is all he says. "You'll always be safe with me."

"So that's why... that's why you brought me here. You didn't kidnap me... you... you saved me."

He nods ever so slightly. "There's still a debt to collect from your father, however. Two, actually."

"You're going to fix what he owes those men?"

"I'm going to protect what is mine."

"And you're not going to hurt him?"

"Do you care about that?"

"We may have a fucked up relationship but he's still my father."

"Yes, of course pretty girl. I won't hurt Dema."

"And you don't expect any kind of *payment* from me right?

"What." His voice drops an octave.

"Umberto . . ."

"Do you honestly want to leave?" He challenges.

He tips to sit forward and pulls something from his back pocket. Umberto offers me his key to the elevator. I don't reach for it, and he places it down on the table between the blueberry muffins and chocolate chip pancakes.

"Go ahead. Leave. You can even have a security detail go with you if you'd like. You'll be safe with them watching you. I'm not even throwing you to the wolves, Victoria. You're free. Fly away if you want to, little bird. Take your cupcake too."

I chuckle a little. "You know you want me to leave the cupcakes, Umberto."

"Fuck yeah, I want you to leave the cupcakes. I didn't say you could take them *all*."

I smile at him, but he just waves me off. "Go ahead. Really."

"Okay."

"Good. Bye."

"Fine."

"Say bye, Victoria."

"Bye. I'm going."

"Why are you still sitting then?"

"Just thinking about how I'm gonna take the cupcakes and not ruin the icing. I mean, I'll leave you the two you finger-fucked to death, but I'm taking the rest."

He bursts out with laughter again as he looks at the poor innocent little cupcakes he ripped all the icing off of as we talked.

"You really are something else, Holt. Damn it." Umberto stands and grabs the key from the table. He walks over to the elevator doors and swipes his key. The doors part instantly because he's made of that kind of magic, and then he grins at me. "I have Tupperware or Ziplock baggies. Pick one."

Is he... is he really challenging me right now? I crack up laughing but then say, "I'd prefer the Tupperware, but that usually requires returning it. So I'll take the Ziplock bag, and I'll be sure to recycle it when I'm done."

I walk to the kitchen, grab the plate of vanilla cupcakes, and shove them at him.

"Fine," he says. Umberto packs up my cupcakes. "Anything else you'd like to take in a doggie bag,

Victoria?" He's too close to me now though. His tight white shirt makes me want to grab hold of him and kiss the hell out of his sexy lips.

No. Hell no. Stop that right now. You're about to be free of this mess. You can leave. He said so. You can leave.

"Nope." I smile up at him and tug the cupcakes out of his hands. "I'm good. I have everything I want, right here." I shake the bag at him, and he growls. It goes right to my most sensitive spots. It's like he knows exactly what to do to turn me on. I swallow hard, and I think he sees that I'm faltering. Umberto steps closer.

"You don't look like you have everything you want, Victoria. Make sure before you leave because once you step through those doors, that's it. You can't come back. I don't do charity work for the same person twice in one lifetime, pretty girl."

Oh hell no, he didn't. "Fuck you, Bova," I spit.

"Try me."

"You wish I would. Don't you?" I step closer and brush the front of his jeans, against the bulge I see poking out. He sucks air through his teeth before he clears his throat.

"Oh, I'm sorry. Did I do that?"

Umberto rips the baggie from my hands and

crashes his lips against mine, tightly gripping my hair as he holds me to him. And I fall. I fall so completely and irrevocably into him that I will never resurface as the same woman I started out as. His kiss has changed from the first time and even from the night we had together. His kiss is pure ownership, pure need, and desire.

I feel his desperation for me to stay. I feel how much he cares and wants me, beyond just my body but the part of me that no one has ever had or ever known before. The real me. The girl I was born to be and have always hidden under the surface out of fear or shame. I don't have to worry about him, and I can finally be free to just live as the woman I am, like the queen I was born to become. I feel like soaring as he wraps me tightly in his arms and deepens our kiss, slowing it down to a crawl so we can truly savor this moment and all the real sweetness it holds, something so much better and more satisfying than the ones I baked.

"Oh, Umberto," I sigh between our kisses.

He groans. "Baby, bring those fucking lips back over here."

We stumble and fall, sending a pile of baking sheet pans I had not yet put away crashing to the floor as he lifts me up on the counter and spreads my legs. I arch my back and let my eyes roll back in my head as I feel him pull my panties to the side and shove his tongue inside of me. He eats me out until I beg for mercy, and then sweeps me roughly into his arms. Kissing me all the way to his room.

I haven't been in his room yet. The door requires his fingerprint, and he fumbles around for the pad to press, making me laugh and forcing him to break our kiss in order to get it right.

"Fucking piece of shit thing," he growls.

"Slow down," I giggle, kissing his cheek.

The door unlocks, and he does anything but slow down, which only makes me laugh harder. We land on the bed, and he crawls over me, kissing my stomach and neck as he murmurs sweetly in my ear.

"Tell me your mine. Say it, Victoria. I need you to say it."

"Mmm, Umberto, I'm yours. I'm all yours. I feel like my truest self with you."

He kisses me hard. "I'm yours if you want me, Victoria Holt."

"I want you so badly," I whisper. "All of you."

"Baby," he dips to my neck and kisses a line right down to my breasts, ripping away my top and exposing my bare tits to him. I arch my back and beg for him to suck on my nipples because his lips are heavenly. My nipples are naturally sensitive, and I love having my tits sucked on, but no one has ever really done it like he does, grabbing hold of both of my breasts, mashing them tightly together and going from one side to the other, sucking hard as he teases me with his perfect white teeth. I could almost come from him toying with me in this way.

"Fuck me. Please. Now. I want you inside of me so badly, baby."

"Fuck yes, Victoria. God, when you beg like that, you turn me rock fucking hard."

I push his jeans away with my hands and then pump him in my hand. He leans in and kisses my mouth, pushing me back down to the plush pillows under my head before he thrusts his hips forward, piercing me with his big cock. And damn, I almost forgot how big he is until he is fully seated inside of me and fucking me hard, giving me all he's got.

I take him to the hilt and cry out from how good it feels every time he hits my G-spot like he has a map to it no other man I've had sex with has ever possessed before. I push at his shoulders, and he complies, letting me up as we keep our lips locked together.

"What do you want, love?" he whispers.

"I want to ride you." I shove him down, and he

laughs as he pulls me onto his hips as he lies back. His dick is so thick and hard as I take him in my hand and guide him to my entrance. I sink easily down on his cock and cry out as he fills me up, stretching me with his girth.

"Fuck baby," he groans, gripping my hips his fingers. "You're so tight and wet."

I bounce on him, swiveling my hips and allowing my clit to slide up and down across his lower stomach, those beautiful rippling abs that are so hot. My hands palm his strong chest as it heaves. Umberto twists his fingers up in my hair, grabbing a thick section as if it were a rope and pulls my neck back, exposing my skin to his mouth to be devoured in hot wet kisses before moving his grip to my tits.

We both come hard and with each other, and as our high tries to find its way back down to Earth, Umberto lands the most tender and delicate kiss on my lips, brushing my hair away from my sweaty face.

"I love you," Umberto whispers sweetly. His eyes so light and sparkling compared to how they are usually dark and mysterious. It feels like when the rain clouds pull away, and you can finally see and feel the warmth from the sun again. Like a spell cast over him has vanished.

This has been a world wind. This is crazy. This

is too soon. But I can barely breathe as tears fill my eyes. Warmth overpowers my heart, and there's a tightness in my chest that I welcome from how much happiness I feel at the moment.

It is what it is.

My feelings are my feelings.

And it doesn't work to try and make any sense of it at all.

"Oh, Umberto, I love you too. You saved me. You're the only person who has ever done that. You're the only one who knows the real me. I belong to you."

"And I'm yours now too, pretty girl. All of me."

He slams his mouth on mine so possessively it makes my heart soar. It's as if I've just given him the greatest gift he has ever had.

What he doesn't realize is it's the best gift I have been given too, because never in my entire life have those three words ever been sweeter.

EPILOGUE

Victoria

Put it between my hands and squeeze. *Oh my God, it's so big, and it moves so damn fast between my fingers, not to mention it is super freaking slippery when wet.*

Oh, why did I think I was cut out for this when clearly, I am not an Italian chick. Now, don't get me wrong. I've handled Umberto's sausage a thousand times, all of which have been perfect and without any kind of screw-ups, but handling Italian sausage like this? Making it from scratch?

Oh, hell no. This is for the birds.

Umberto laughs as he watches me.

"Oh, you think it's funny, do you? You try it then."

"It is easy," he says, still grinning at me. Looking like a million damn dollars in his designer suit and perfectly chaotic mess of hair on top of his sexy head. "But I don't dare to touch a damn thing in this place."

"Awe, baby, are you scared of your grandma?"

"Damn right, I'm scared of my grandma. Do you see those huge wooden spoons on the wall? They are not for decoration. If you look closely at my ass, you can still see the impressions from where she hit me as a child."

"I'm sure you deserved it."

"Oh, I definitely fucking deserved it," he grins again. "But that's not the point."

"Well, why don't you leave the kitchen to us then, and you go back to whatever it is you do around here that won't get your ass kicked by an old lady." I tip up on my toes and kiss him.

"Whatever you say," he whispers, kissing me back tenderly, "Mrs. Bova."

He smacks my ass like it's a stamp of his face on my backside as he walks away. I just chuckle at him and then get back to trying to perfect Grandma Bova's insanely good homemade sausage recipe.

Umberto and I have been married for three years now. I love him so much it's insane. This ruthless gangster to everyone else has found a soft spot in his soul for me, and I have made a home for him inside of the girl who has never trusted a single person in her life. Until now.

Together we are trying to change who we used to be and find out who we are together. There is no secret too big or a burden that we have to carry on our own. We take it one day at a time, and we find our pace as we go.

He's trying to slowly become more legit in his business endeavors, especially in the food businesses. With me at his side helping out and actually living out some of my biggest dreams too.

It turns out medical school and becoming a doctor wasn't something that I really had my heart set on. It was something I thought I wanted because of a moment in my childhood that made me feel empowered. A rarity in my old world.

The girl who could not even stand up for herself to have a place to study in her dorm room is not the woman I am today. The woman who worked hide to hide from the notoriety and shame of her parents sins is not the woman I am today.

No.

The woman who exists now is Victoria Michelle Bova. I made my own history and name for myself in this city. In the last three years, I have become a woman who is to be treated with respect, and it is because I have earned it as a chef and smart businesswoman.

I am a woman who gives back to my community and takes pride in my work. I associate with people that I actually enjoy being around and not just people that can get me the kind of connections and association a soulless person would attack like a vulture going for an easy meal.

The kind of life that I want to live is one filled with meaningful, loving moments that last forever and aren't just there to look good in front of speculating eyes. I want to be better than my parents and give more back to my life and my marriage than what I witnessed as a kid.

That is not what I want for a child of my own. I want to give them a life where they know they are loved without question. Where they know that they are the most important things. More than this place. More than money. More than fame. More than my own life. And in order to do that, I had to learn the power of forgiving and letting go of the past. I cannot allow myself to be controlled by it anymore.

When I sparkle and shine looking at my husband, it's because no one makes me feel as loved or special as he does. There is not another soul on the planet that has ever cherished me the way he does or goes out of his way to treat me daily like I am a queen standing beside him. And likewise, there is nothing phony about my love for him.

I don't love him for his money or power. I love him for being the kind of man that once had the chance to get back what was his and decided to gain something more valuable in its place. He traded money for love, his life for mine, and I don't know if there is anything more selfless or loving in the entire universe than that.

Umberto showed me that no matter how you start out your life, there is always more than one route to take and when the road you are on is heading in a bad direction you have the right as the person in the driver's seat to take it a different course and change your destination.

You don't need some weird boss lady telling you that your name is Destiny in order to believe it. You just have to make up your mind to allow love to lead your path and follow it where it may go. Because you just never know how love can change things in your life until you decide to be brave enough and give it a try.

I'm so fucking glad I did.

Umberto

There are so many times during the day when I glance at my wife Victoria and wonder how the fuck I got so damn lucky. How could a girl like her ever love someone like me? She is the light in my world of darkness. A ray of blinding sunshine.

I walk with men that don't even have souls, yet somehow, this angel belongs to me. How? I don't fucking know, but I spend every second of my time with her making sure she fucking knows how much I love and adore her. I make sure she is fully fucking aware of the effect she has on me, and even though it kills me to share with her the kind of shit I've done and have that on the table, I know she is the one person I can trust not to betray me. And that feeling is fucking everything when you're a dead man that people still want to kill over and over again, for just existing.

I watch her as she cooks in one of our newest business ventures. She's so damn hot. And everything just seems to come so easily to her. There was no way that I could live, not knowing her life wasn't good, that she wasn't completely fucking happy, completely safe. She looks pretty damn happy. In fact her happiness is pretty damn blinding.

I didn't grow up a happy kid. I grew up running deals for my father even though I didn't know anything about it at the time. I was groomed from a young age just by being around the fucking guy.

Like when he'd pick me up from my mom's house on the weekend and then take me to one of his many mistresses' houses. That's where he hid his shit before he blew up big on the streets. So I'd have to hide in the closet and wait for him to, uh, finish, his little ventures before we got to go for a slice in the city.

Even that was deal-making though. Every spot seemed to know my father's name. They never ask him for money, but they always fucking had some to hand over. Everything was free. Everything was offered to him at the best quality and with a smile, even if it was forced. They feared him. I wanted that feeling. I thought that was the measure of true success in life.

I caught a glimpse of what my father really did when I was about fifteen years old. It was the first time I had ever been tasked to handle some shit for the clique he ran. I was scared shitless, even though I tried to act brave with balls of brass. I wanted him to be proud of me and not think I was some pussy little punk that could not handle my shit, even though that's exactly what I felt like then. I had to beat the snot out of a guy who owed the clique money. I was naturally a lot bigger than most men, even guys that were twice my age, standing at six foot one.

After I beat the shit out of the guy who owed us money, my father finally looked at me as if he saw me for the first time in my life. I clung to that feeling, and every job after that was a thoughtless venture that required only my fists and no brains. But before all of that, I didn't understand that I had to back a motherfucker up off me with deadly force if I wanted to be respected fully by the clique, or by anyone.

My mother was not a good person either. A lot of it wasn't her fault though. She was ruined by my father in ways that I guess only she could tell you about, but I saw a lot of the shit go down. I saw the fights and heard the screaming. I heard her yell at him, and that's how I learned all the bad words in Italian. I learned what a *whore* was in Italian because that's what she was mainly always screaming about.

When my father finally left, it was like a hole was left wide open in my house, and my mother had to figure out how to fill it up with something new. So I had a lot of stepfathers and new "uncles" I had never met before.

My 'Uncle Joe' was a man that I would, later on, grow up to kill. He was my first hit, and I didn't need orders because when I was eight years old, Uncle Joe liked to get drunk and beat the fuck out of my mom before turning on me. He had a thick leather belt and used it liberally. I learned how to be brutal from him. I learned how to make killing the same as breathing. So easy you don't even think about it.

There are so many times when I'm holding on to Victoria, and I place my hands against her ribs,

feeling her life flow in and out of her lungs, and I
think to myself; she has no idea how easily I could
end a person. She has no idea about the kind of
monster she has quieted. I don't think about it
anymore. I don't let that side of me have a place
inside of my bones. But damn, when he did, he was
fucking ruthless.

I try to float on the surface of shit now. I let what
people already know do the talking for me before I
ever have to lay a finger on them. It's usually enough.
I am glad for that. I don't want to be my father
anymore, which is a relief greater than I could
describe because, for my entire life, that was my
whole purpose in life.

Closing the curtain on the past and trying to
build something new and brighter is what I live for
these days. Don't get me wrong, I'm willing and able
to fuck a person up on sight if they step the fuck out
of line, but I'm trying to live in a way where I won't
ever have to do it out of need. There are times I feel
that monster trying to rattle my cage and be set free.
Like when Victoria walks through the dining room
and makes sure everyone is satisfied with their food
and a dense table of pricks wants to eye her like she's
on the menu. That kind of shit makes the monster

inside of me fucking livid. And if they ever tried anything beyond roaming their eyes over her, I'd light the fucking room on fire. Even though I fully understand and agree with it.

She is always the hottest woman in the room. Even when she isn't trying. Her moonlit hued skin and distractible eyes. The confident way she handles herself. Fuck, that is the sexiest thing about her. Her strength and kindness.

I used to think showing kindness was a sign of weakness, but now I get it. I understand how powerful it can be. But those men aren't exactly looking at her from that point of view, and that's what lights me up so fucking bad. They only see great tits and an ass. They are too dumb to believe a woman like her would not be taken by a crazy motherfucker like me who would brutally commit a million crimes, nothing short of murder, before he would ever allow another man to come anywhere near her. She's mine, goddamnit.

The beast in me wants to roar the words like a fierce lion protecting his pride. I have to take a deep breath just to keep my ass in my seat, but I swear my hand is always ready on my Glock that I keep tucked beneath my jacket, just in fucking case a motherfucker thinks about acting stupid.

Tonight she's dressed in a simple black dress under her matching black apron with her hair piled up into a pretty bun on her head with a few stray curls that fall against the back of her neck.

I love that look on her, with her neck exposed. I feel like fucking Satan in that classic fucking movie with Keanu Reeves, Devil's Advocate, when Lucifer decides to pull up Charlize's hair and show her how fucking sexy she is with nothing surrounding her face. In the movie, it was to deceive the girl about her looks and make her into something only he desires, but in my world with Victoria, it is the truth.

She is fucking brutally hot with her hair off her shoulders like that because her skin is flawless and as soft as crushed velvet. I get hard just thinking about touching her. The smell of her. The scent of her spicy skin mixed with her vanilla lotion, and how it feels nude underneath me as she cries out my name. Fuck.

I have to get myself together. Taxes. I look back at the paper on the table. Yes. If anything is going to make me lose a raging hard on for my wife it is definitely going to be motherfucking taxes.

She comes over to me as I sit in the corner booth and go over numbers. Yeah, I do that kind of shit now too. Pay taxes. For fuck's sake. I should just grow a pair of tits while I'm at it.

"Hey pretty girl." I reach up and kiss her, grabbing her ass a little just to let those motherfuckers know what's up. She flushes as she kisses me back.

"I brought you some dinner." She sets a steaming bowl of seafood pasta down and kisses me again before she sidles up beside me. "How's it looking, babe?"

"You know who the real mob is, love? The fucking IRS. The shakedown I'm suffering right now, Victoria, is so fucking real it kills me not be able to retaliate. If anyone has ever deserved a... fuck, I won't even finish that sentence in your presence. Forgive me. But it would not be pretty if I ever had to sit down with one of these fucking guys. Just know that. Not at fucking all."

She laughs, and that is what quiets the beast the most.

"Babe, you're crazy, but I love you." She palms my cheek and kisses me again. I kiss her back, and she giggles as I try to go a hell of a lot further than kosher in a setting like this. She leans her head on my chest. "Yes, I definitely love you, Umberto."

I lied. Her confession is what quiets the beast inside of me the most. It practically kills him.

"I love you, doll. More than anything in the whole fucking world do I love you."

Her eyes sparkle as she stares up at me. I put my hand under her chin and press the pad of my thumb to the apple of her cheek, soothing her skin as I wonder quietly.

"How the fuck did I get you, college girl? How did I get so damn lucky when I have so much to repent for? A sinner like me?"

Ignoring where we are, my girl cups the back up my head and pulls me into her for a heated kiss.

I whisper against her lips. "I'm about to shut this whole place down if you don't stop that, love."

"Oh, Umberto," she sighs. Victoria reaches up and takes my hand from her cheek, sliding it down her body. I think for a moment she's actually going to play along with me and let me get away with some shit like this in the restaurant, but she takes my hand and rests it on her stomach, pressing my palm firmly against her body.

"I'm feeling just a little extra emotional today."

"Why, babe?" I worry for a second. Did something happen? "Are you okay?"

"I'm fine," she smiles. "I'm pregnant. We're going to have a baby."

Her eyes seem unsure at first, and then she smiles this brilliant smile that's more blinding than anything I have ever witnessed in my life. It does fucked-up shit to my heart that makes my damn chest hurt. I feel like a mack truck is bulldozing its way inside of my chest, and I can't stop it from happening. What's more confusing is that I don't even want to. That feeling fills me up to a point of completion. Paying taxes and living legit seems like child's play in comparison to that feeling.

"Umberto, say something," she says with lines of worry spreading across her forehead. "Please."

I blink, and it's then I realize there's something wet in my eyes. I have to clear my throat just to form a damn sentence and the only thing that comes to mind is the truth. The absolute truth about everything and the only thing that carries any weight in my world anymore.

"I love you so fucking much, Victoria. You changed my life. You gave me a life worth living and worth fighting for. That's one thing I was always wrong about. I thought I had to fight everything and everybody in the world in order to win in life, but the only thing I have to really put my life on the line for now, is you, Victoria. You have no idea how much you mean to me, love. But I'm going to live every day of my life trying to become worthy of you." I kiss her. "Of both of you, pretty girl."

"I love you too, so much. You make me so happy. You'll be such a good father. I know you will."

She smiles so beautifully, and tears roll down her face. I hate the fucking sight even though I know she's only crying because she's happy. Still, I wipe her cheeks clean with the pads of my thumbs and kiss her until the feeling in my chest is lighter, like a balloon set on soaring to the clouds. Exactly where I want to be.

I will never allow my child to grow up like we did, completely forgotten and used by our parents for their own selfish gain.

If there is one thing my eyes have been opened to it is the fact that no matter who you were born to become, or what name you were given, you can still choose a different path for yourself and be free to choose something else, something better. You can change it if you decide that your destiny is in another direction, and it is as simple as walking away and walking toward what you really want more than anything else.

I was born Umberto Bova. Son of the Andolini

Crime Family. Don to the Bova familia of that syndicate. Ruthless killer. Soulless judge and jury.

I was born into a clique of gangsters. I was groomed to become the most ruthless bastard in New York, and for the better portion of my life, I was that man.

People still fear me, but these days I don't have a craving for blood. I once joked that I had no friends to call me by my nickname. At the time, that was true. But that was before I met an angel who saved my soul from the pits of hell.

I am now the new and improved Umberto Bova. I am now free. And as long as I am breathing, the woman I love, who is now carrying my child, will be free too.

Ω Ω Ω

Thank you for reading UMBERTO's journey. It is the third novel in the Andolini Crime Family Series, and I hope you enjoyed it. **Grab the entire series at its lowest price or for free on Kindle Unlimited today.**

Please Sign Up To Be Notified when my next release
is live and don't forget to leave a review if you've
enjoyed this novel. I appreciate the encouraging
words more than you know.

You can also chat with me on Facebook.
Or follow me on Instagram.

ALSO BY COCO MILLER

Big City Billionaires
Faking For Mr. Pope
Virgin Escort For Mr. Vaughn
Pretending for Mr. Parker

Red Bratva Billionaires
MAXIM
SERGEI
VIKTOR

The Overwatch Division
WYATT
ASA
CESAR

Andolini Crime Family

CARMINE

GIOVANNI

UMBERTO